Meet the WILD SOUTHWEST

Meet the WILD

LAND OF HOODOOS

SOUTHWEST
AND GILA MONSTERS

SUSAN J. TWEIT
ILLUSTRATIONS BY JOYCE BERGEN

DISCLAIMER: This book is written for youngsters and adults. It is the publisher's hope that children will receive guidance from an adult before pursuing any of the ideas suggested here. Neither the author nor the publisher is responsible for any adverse reactions or injuries individuals might experience from eating wild foods or undertaking activities discussed in this book.

Library of Congress Cataloging-in-Publication Data
Tweit, Susan J.
        Meet the wild Southwest : land of hoodoos and gila monsters / text by Susan J. Tweit ;
illustrations by Joyce Bergen.
        p.   cm.
        Includes bibliographical references and index.
        ISBN 0-88240-468-7 (pbk.)
        1. Natural history —Southwest, New—Juvenile literature.
    2. Desert ecology, Southwest, New—Juvenile literature.
    3. Southwest, New   [1. Natural history—Southwest, New.
    2. Southwest, New—Description and travel.]   I. Bergen, Joyce,
    1949 -   ill.   II. Title.
    QH104.5.S6T85   1995
    508.79—dc20   95-432
                                                                   CIP
                                                                   AC

Originating Editor: Marlene Blessing
Managing Editor: Ellen Harkins Wheat
Editors: Deb Easter and Carolyn Smith
Designer: Kate L. Thompson
Map: Peter Schwab (design) and Joyce Bergen (illustrations)
Illustrations. *Cover:* Collared lizard. *Pages 2–3:* Tarantula and claret cup cactus. *Page 6:* Packrat.

Alaska Northwest Books™
An imprint of Graphic Arts Publishing Company
Editorial office: 2208 NW Market Street, Suite 300, Seattle, WA 98107
Catalog and order dept.: P.O. Box 10306, Portland, OR 97210
800-452-3032

Printed on recycled paper in the United States of America

DEDICATION

This book is for Blanche and Dia, two of my favorite kids, and for Karla and the folks at Canyonlands Field Institute, who not only care about the landscape and cultures of the Colorado Plateau, but are dedicating themselves to its future for the kid in all of us.

A portion of the royalties from this book will go to support the nonprofit Canyonlands Field Institute, P.O. Box 68, Moab, UT 84532, phone (801) 259-8850.

The mission of Canyonlands Field Institute is to promote understanding, appreciation, and stewardship of the natural environment and cultural heritage of the Colorado Plateau. Through educational programs for children and adults, Canyonlands Field Institute encourages informed individual action and public decision-making that support a sustainable future for the Colorado Plateau and the earth as a whole.

ACKNOWLEDGMENTS

Thanks to Molly, who inspired me to remember the wonder of discovery. Thanks to Marlene Blessing for believing in this project through its various metamorphoses; to Carolyn Smith for her sensitive, thoughtful, and thorough editorial vision; to Deb Easter for keeping me thinking like a kid; to Mary Ross for laughter and instruction in the Zen of marketing and sales; and to Ellen Wheat for managing this project. Thanks to Kate Thompson for designing a more wonderful book than I imagined, and to Joyce Bergen for the beautiful, whimsical, and incredibly well-researched illustrations. Thanks also to Joan Tweit and Doris Evans for patiently checking the facts and reminding me how to read like a kid. And special thanks to Jayne Belnap for elucidating the wonders of cryptobiotic crusts.

This book would never have happened without the support and encouragement of my family, Richard and Molly Cabe, and my parents, Robert and Joan Tweit. Many friends and colleagues shared my enthusiasm and patiently answered my queries—thanks to you all. Any errors or omissions are, of course, my own responsibility.

Contents

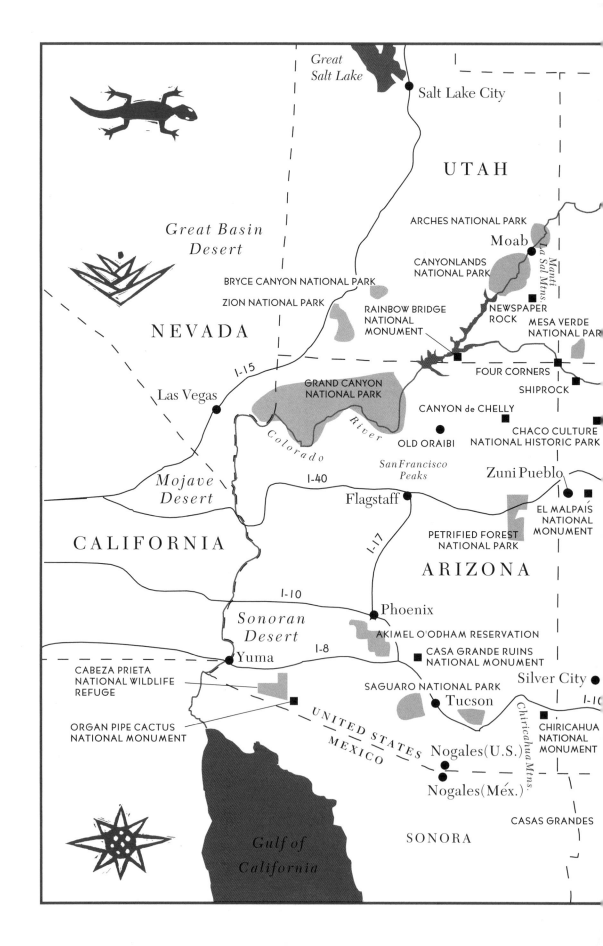

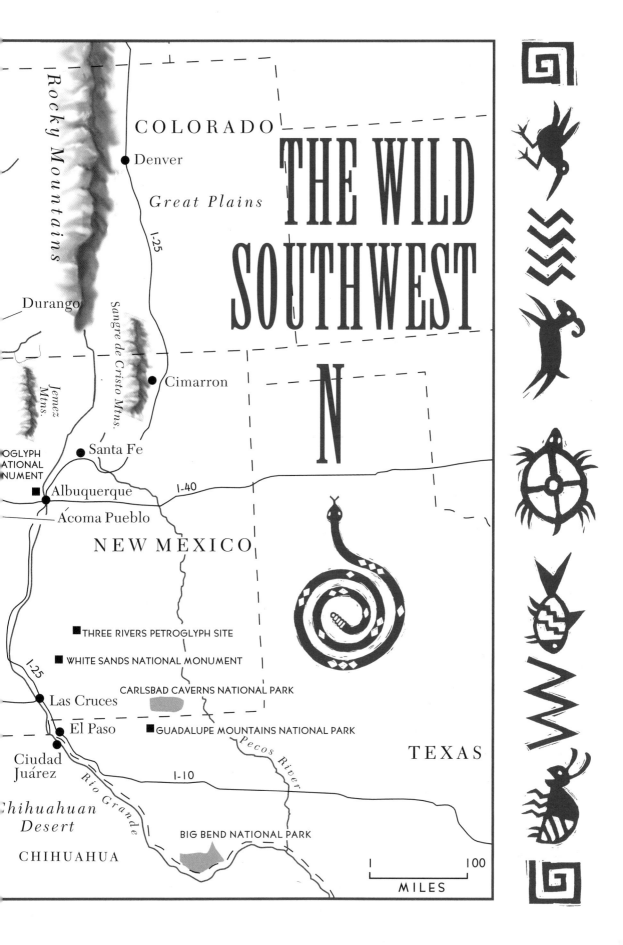

The Wild Sout

THE SOUTHWEST IS A LAND OF EXTREMES, ranging from high mountains to deserts at sea level. It can be unbearably hot or terribly cold. In fact, one Southwest county, San Juan County, Utah, boasts one of the widest temperature ranges in the world,

LAND OF EXTREMES

from summer highs of 115 degrees Fahrenheit to winter lows of 29 degrees below zero. "Dry" defines the Southwest, but two of western North America's largest rivers drain the region. Amazingly, drowning is a common cause of death in this land of little rain.

The region called the Southwest means different things to different people. In this book, I use ecological and cultural connections to define the Southwest as all of New Mexico and Arizona, southern Utah, southwestern Colorado, and far west Texas. Because so much of the landscape, culture, and history of parts of adjacent northern Mexico are joined to the American Southwest, I've included it in this book as well.

The first part of the book describes the basics of the Southwest—geology, climate, and plants and animals. Then, to help you understand the relationships between the region's special plants, animals, and natural features, I've divided the book into thematic chapters, such as

HOW TO ENJOY THE SOUTHWEST

Bring a respectful attitude to the Southwest. Watch animals, but don't disturb them by picking them up or by disturbing their homes. Admire plants, but don't pick flowers or uproot them. Look at rock drawings and other artifacts of ancient people, but leave them be. As a sign in the cathedral in Santa Fe, New Mexico, says, "This is a sacred place. Please behave accordingly."

west

"Plants and Romance" or "Splendid Soarers." These chapters explore questions like, How do Southwest animals and plants live? Talk? Eat? How do the region's peoples and creatures survive in such a hot, dry climate? Why does the Southwest have so many rocky canyons? Throughout these chapters I've included weird and interesting facts, fun stuff to do, and tips on where to find Southwestern things that you've read about in the book.

At the back of the book, I've included a write-up of some of the Southwest's endangered species, a list of local museums and zoos with exhibits on natural history and cultural heritage, a selection of my favorite books about the Southwest, a checklist so you can keep track of what you've seen, and a glossary of terms. And if you are looking for a specific animal, plant, place, or phenomenon, check the index at the back of the book.

Horned lizard in Monument Valley, Arizona

SOUTHWEST FACTS

- The Southwest includes all four North American deserts: the Sonoran, the Chihuahuan, the Mojave, and the Great Basin.

- More kinds of rattlesnakes live in the Southwest than anywhere else in North America, but you are more likely to be struck by lightning in the Southwest than bitten by a rattlesnake.

- The only spot in the United States where you can stand in four states at once is in the Southwest, at Four Corners, where Utah, Colorado, New Mexico, and Arizona meet.

- North America's deepest canyon, the mile-deep Grand Canyon in Arizona, is in the Southwest.

- The Southwest includes the world's fifth-longest cave, 182-mile-long Lechuguilla Cave in Carlsbad Caverns National Park, New Mexico.

- The Southwest is home to the two oldest towns in the United States: Ácoma Pueblo in central New Mexico, and Old Oraibi, in the Hopi Reservation of northern Arizona. Both were founded over 900 years ago.

Geology

ONCE, MUCH OF THE SOUTHWEST was covered with water—salt water. Over millions of years, shallow seas repeatedly flooded the region and then retreated. The shells of sea animals, from tiny plankton to giant horseshoe crabs, sank to the sea

ONCE UPON A TIME . . .

bottom, gradually building layers of muck. Waves deposited sand along the beaches. In the quiet waters of swamps and marshes, rivers dropped mud and gravel. On land lived small, graceful dinosaurs and dragonflies with 3-foot wingspans.

As the seas advanced and retreated across the Southwest, new sediments were dropped atop old ones. The weight of the new layers hardened the old layers into rock. Sea-bottom mud became limestone. Sands hardened to sandstone. Marsh mud became shales. For a time, a salty lake many times larger than Utah's Great Salt Lake covered part of the Southwest. Later, dry sand dunes stretched for miles and miles across the northern Southwest. These too left layers of sediments that were slowly buried and pressed into layers of rock. (In places on the Colorado Plateau, you can still see slanting lines of the "fossil" dunes and the ripple marks made by ancient winds.)

Around 65 million years ago, most of the plant-eating dinosaurs and other ancient life died out, probably because a meteor shower lasting hundreds of years bombarded the earth. Later, the earth's crust all across what is now the western part of the United States began to buckle, rip, and stretch. In the Southwest, mountains and plateaus were pushed upward, valleys dropped downward, thick layers of solid rock were bent into great folds, and volcanoes belched forth huge clouds of ash and flows of lava.

Around two million years ago, the beginning of the Ice Age cooled the Southwest. Enormous plant-eating animals were dominant, including huge, furry mastodons bigger than today's elephants, giant camels, and three-quarter-ton armadillos.

Today, the giant plant-eaters are gone, perhaps killed off around 11,000 years ago by early human migrants to

HOT TIP!

Rock collecting is illegal at most parks. But Rockhound State Park near Deming, New Mexico, was set up just for rock collectors. Look for beautiful agates (multicolored quartz) and geodes (rocks with crystals inside).

Geode

ROCK FACTS

- One of the oldest rocks in the Southwest is Vishnu schist, a two-billion-year-old dark rock visible at the bottom of the Grand Canyon.

- The Guadalupe Mountains on the border of Texas and New Mexico are actually ancient ocean reefs built millions of years ago in shallow seawater by coral and other sea animals. Carlsbad Caverns and other caves are eroded into the ancient reefs.

- The world's largest concentration of petrified tree trunks— trees that have turned into rock—stick out of shale badlands at Petrified Forest National Park in northern Arizona. Layers of mud and ash from erupting volcanoes killed and buried the trees. Instead of rotting, the wood slowly turned to colorful agate.

- Around 1,000 years ago, a volcano near Grants, New Mexico, leaked lava, flooding a valley at what is now El Malpaís National Monument. Navajo origin stories say that the black rock is dried blood from a giant slain by the Hero Twins as they made *Diné Tah*, Navajoland, safe for their people.

- The world's finest dinosaur tracks can be found in the Robledo Mountains near Las Cruces, New Mexico. Footprints from dozens of kinds of dinosaurs and other early animals crisscross rocks hardened from 250-million-year-old mudflats.

Dinosaur tracks

the Southwest. The Southwest is still shaped by wind and water. But people have a great and rapid impact on the landscape too. We build dams, submerging beautiful canyons and valleys. We level whole mountains to mine copper. Our roads and cities pave the landscape, destroying other creatures' homes. We use water faster than rivers and streams can replenish it. We have much to learn.

Climate

THE SOUTHWEST IS DRY for much of the year. High mountain ranges to the west block the Southwest from the Pacific Ocean, the West's great rain factory. Rain does come in summer, brought by wet south winds.

HOW DRY? HOW HOT? And what rain! Lightning flashes, thunder booms, and sheets of water fall to the ground. Soon, the rain stops and the sun is out again. In some parts of the Southwest, rain—or snow—also falls in the winter.

Rainfall varies with elevation. As moist air rises to pass over high plateaus or mountains, the air cools, causing its load of moisture to condense and to fall as rain or snow. Thus, lower elevations are much dryer than higher elevations. For instance, Yuma, Arizona, one of the lowest points in the Southwest at 137 feet above sea level, averages only 4 inches of moisture per year, while the Southwest's high mountains may receive 35 inches a year, nearly nine times as much.

Yuma is often the hottest town in the United States. Summer days in Yuma can sizzle at 128 degrees F, hot enough to fry an egg on the ground! But temperatures grow cooler as you go uphill. For every thousand feet of elevation gain, average temperatures drop four degrees. So, on a summer afternoon at Phantom Ranch in the bottom of the Grand Canyon, the high may be 100 degrees, while 5,500 feet above at Bright Angel Point on the canyon's North Rim, the thermometer will read only 80 degrees.

> **HOT TIP!**
>
> The sun is strong in the Southwest, even when the weather is not hot. To protect yourself, use sunscreen (with an SPF rating of at least 20), and wear a hat and sunglasses all the time.

DEATH IN THE DESERT

In hot, dry climates, if you don't drink enough water (at least a gallon a day), you can get dehydrated and feel dizzy, sick, or exhausted—or even die. Always carry a gallon of water per person per day on hikes because you can't count on finding water in the desert. Almost every year, someone dies of dehydration in the Southwest.

Plants and Animals

OVER THE AGES, an amazing assortment of plants and animals have lived in the Southwest, from ferns as tall as trees, to dinosaurs that stretched 150 feet nose to tail, to beavers the size of Volkswagen Beetles. Who lives in the region now? A weird

WHO LIVES HERE?

and wonderful variety, from tiny bacteria between grains of sand in dunes, to 150-foot-tall ponderosa pine trees and 300-pound black bears.

No one knows exactly how many species—distinct kinds— of animals and plants live in the Southwest. Biologists estimate that *20,000* species of insects, spiders, and other arthropods—animals with jointed legs and no backbones—live in New Mexico alone, along with 149 species of mammals, 400 species of birds, 61 species of fish, and 122 species of reptiles and amphibians! And 3,500 species of plants live in Arizona alone.

SURVIVING IN THE DESERT

Desert plants and animals must survive months and months with no rain. Some, including both cacti and desert tortoises, store water inside their body, like having internal water bottles. Many plants coat their leaves with wax to slow water loss. Some do without leaves altogether. Other plants, like sego lilies, hide underground as bulbs and sprout only when conditions are right. Others survive as seeds, which sprout when rainfall and temperature are just right.

When things grow too dry or too hot, some larger desert animals simply leave for cooler places. But others, like horned lizards or tarantula spiders, cannot move away. They stay out of the hot sun and are active only in the cooler nights. Some desert animals, like kangaroo rats, get all their moisture from the food they eat and never need to drink water!

Desert tortoise

HOT TIP!

The best time to see animals when the weather is hot is in the cool early morning or late evening. In winter, warm afternoons are the most rewarding times to look for wildlife.

Each plant and animal is adapted to a particular set of conditions, or habitat. Climate—how hot or cold it is, how dry or wet—is one of the most important conditions defining habitat. Very different animals and plants live at the lowest elevations of the Southwest, in the hot deserts, than in the cold, moist conditions at the highest mountaintops.

The deserts support a sparse cover of plants like spiny cacti, wiry shrubs and small trees, and tough bunches of grass. Here live tarantulas, scorpions, roadrunners, and other animals able to handle heat and drought. Going uphill, rainfall increases and the desert gradually changes to grassland dotted with plants like agaves and ocotillos. Here live animals like grasshoppers, horned lizards, burrowing owls, and pronghorn antelope.

Farther uphill in the foothills, mesas, and dry mountain slopes, trees grow—scattered junipers, oaks, and piñon pines, with grasses underneath. Here live animals such as western bluebirds, wood rats, and mountain lions. Still farther uphill, enough rain falls to nourish forests of tall ponderosa pines, and aspen, spruce, and fir. Here,

mountains and high plateaus form sky islands—cool, moist environments high above the deserts. Sky islands shelter animals that cannot survive heat and drought, including salamanders, kingsnakes, snowshoe hares, and black bears.

Where permanent water flows, oases dot the Southwest. The water of springs, marshes, ponds, streams, and rivers nourishes dense plant growth, from tall cottonwood trees to thick stands of cattails. Such "jungles" house more wildlife per square foot than any other Southwest habitat. Here live dragonflies, frogs, turtles, kingfishers, river otters, and other animals that need a permanent supply of water.

Can you guess the most common large animal in the Southwest? People!

ANIMAL FACTS

■ Pupfish are chubby, minnow-like fish that live only in isolated desert springs and streams. They can survive in water up to five times as salty as seawater and as hot as 112 degrees F.

■ Desert tortoises, plant-eaters native to the hot Sonoran and Mojave deserts, can store up to a cup of water in their bladder to "drink" during dry times. In some places, housing developments endanger these long-lived creatures by destroying their desert habitat.

■ Peccaries are piglike animals native to the foothills of the southern Southwest and northern Mexico. Though their eyesight is poor, they have a keen sense of smell. Peccaries travel in small packs and "talk" to each other with smells emitted by the musk glands on their rump.

Peccaries

Land

of Hoodoos and Gila Monsters

Spiny Survivors

CACTI ARE ODD PLANTS. They are covered with spines. Cactus stems swell with water after rains, and shrink as the plant drinks its stores. Tough, waxy skin protects cacti against water loss and sunburn (plants sunburn too!). They come in all shapes and sizes—some cacti are short and round, some are tall as trees, some grow in dense clusters, some are many-branched like shrubs. These forbidding plants produce gorgeous flowers, with satiny, bright-colored petals.

SAGUARO
PRICKLY PEAR
CHOLLA

Prickly pear cactus

Cholla cactus

Cacti evolved—gradually changed—from a group of roselike plants as the climate of the Southwest grew warmer and drier beginning about 50 million years ago. As the climate warmed, the plants changed in order to survive desert conditions—hot temperatures and lack of water. Cacti evolved ways to store water in their cells and fleshy stems. Instead of water-hungry leaves, cacti have spines, which don't evaporate water and lose less heat than plant leaves. Today there are 1,200 species of cacti. They are native only to North and South America.

Saguaros (say sa-WAH-rows) are North America's tallest cacti. These giants grow as tall as 50 feet and are native to the Sonoran Desert in Arizona and northern Sonora, Mexico. Saguaros may sprout a dozen thick branches and weigh several tons—as much as a small elephant! They grow very slowly, taking 25 to 50 years to reach 6 feet tall, living as long as 200 years.

Saguaros bloom in May, producing clusters of big, vase-shaped white flowers at the ends of their stems. The flowers open at night. Their smell and white color attract flocks of bats, which slurp

the blossoms' nectar and pollinate them. The sweet, scarlet pulp of saguaro fruits is devoured by desert insects, birds, and other animals. In early summer, the Tohono O'odham, Sonoran Desert Native Americans, call up the summer rains by drinking wine fermented from saguaro fruits.

Prickly pears and chollas are shrubby cacti with branching stems of many "pads" or "joints." The two are closely related, but look quite different. Prickly pear pads are flat and oval-shaped, like beaver tails. Cholla joints are rounded and shaped like a tube. These cacti spread when the sharp spines of their easily broken-off pads or joints stick on unwary passersby. Wherever they are dropped, the joints take root and grow new plants. The whitish, cottony patches sometimes found on prickly pear and cholla cacti are colonies of cochineal bugs—small, sap-sucking insects that eat cactus juices.

Many other kinds of cacti live in the Southwest. Look for fishhook cacti, small cacti named for their fishhook-shaped spines and barrel cacti, stout, unbranching cacti named for their shape.

HOT TIP!

To pull out sharp cactus spines, use a pair of pliers or a comb. (If the spines are hooked, catch the hooked end between the teeth of a comb and pull.)

YOU CAN DO IT! Southwesterners eat prickly pear cacti. The pads, or nopalitos (say no-pah-LEE-toes), are peeled and steamed as a vegetable. The sweet fruits, called tunas (TOO-nahs), can be eaten raw (peel off the skin and spines first), or boiled and made into jellies and syrups. To gather your own tunas: look for the ripe purple fruits and pick them with kitchen tongs to avoid the spines. Carefully peel the skin and clusters of spines, then eat the sweet, soft insides.

HOME IN THE SPINES Many desert creatures, from insects to owls, live in cacti. Gila woodpeckers and gilded flickers dig nest holes in saguaro trunks and arms. These holes are later used by other birds and animals, from tiny elf owls to snakes. Cactus wrens and curve-billed thrashers build their nests in cholla cactus, protected by a fortress of sharp spines.

Saguaro cactus

Fishhook cactus spine

Bat in flight

Plants and Romance

MOST ANIMALS REPRODUCE by finding and mating with a member of the opposite sex. Plants, however, are rooted in place. They can't move about and find mates. How do they reproduce? In flowering plants, flowers are where sex happens. The pollen, contained in sacs on stalks within the flower, must reach the ovules, the flower's unfertilized eggs, which are hidden inside the pistil at the center of the flower. When the pollen reaches the ovule, a fertile seed is formed. That seed is the plant's child. Flowering plants use various tricks to get pollen to the ovule.

AGAVE
YUCCA

Some plants grow tiny, plain flowers, with no petals or bright colors. Grasses, cottonwoods, and pine trees are in this group. They depend on the wind to move their pollen from flower to flower. Their stamens are specially designed to vibrate in the slightest breeze, loosing blizzards of feather-light pollen grains to float on the air.

Other plants depend on insects, birds, or bats to transport their pollen from flower to flower. These plants attract animal pollinators by producing nectar—food—for the animals to eat, and advertise with brightly colored, fancily shaped flowers. As the diners move from flower to flower,

they carry pollen from one flower's pollen sacs to another flower's pistil. Flowers that open at night lure hungry fliers with sweet smells and light-colored petals.

Sexual reproduction takes a lot of energy. So some plants, like aspens, simply make a clone, a new plant identical to the parent. There are dangers, though, to cloning yourself. See *Look-Alikes* on page 46 for more details.

HOW BATS HELP PLANTS REPRODUCE On a warm May night in the southern Southwest, flower buds open on a 10-foot-tall flower stalk. If you could stand on a stepladder and smell the flowers, you would be surprised—they stink like rotting meat. These are agave flowers. Their odor, unpleasant to humans, attracts night-flying bats. The bats circle the flower stalk, hovering, and one by one move in to feed on flower nectar. As a hovering bat shoves its slender snout into the flower to drink, its fur is dusted with pollen. When the bat flies on to another flower to feed, pollen from its fur sticks to the flower's pistil. Food for the bat, reproduction for the agave.

FOOD FOR MY BROOD Sometimes mistaken for agaves, yuccas also sprout tall flower stalks in the spring and summer. But agaves only bloom once in their lifetime; yuccas bloom every year. Yuccas' sweet-smelling, ivory-colored flowers hang down like bells. Each species of yucca attracts its own species of moth. A female yucca moth gathers pollen from a yucca flower and works it into a tiny ball before flying to another flower. She stuffs the pollen ball into the new flower's pistil, thus fertilizing its eggs, then lays her own eggs there too. The growing yucca seeds provide food for her brood of grublike larvae, and the larvae leave some seeds to grow into new yuccas.

Bat drinking nectar from a saguaro blossom

Winged Wonders

HUMMINGBIRDS AND SPHINX MOTHS BOTH HOVER, and both sip nectar from flowers. But these two Southwest residents are as different as day and night: hummingbirds fly during the daytime, whereas sphinx moths take the night shift.

HUMMINGBIRDS
SPHINX MOTHS
DRAGONFLIES

Southwest hummingbirds include North America's tiniest bird, the 2¾-inch-long calliope hummingbird, which weighs about as much as a penny; and the 5-plus-inch-long blue-throated hummingbird, one of the largest hummingbirds. Whatever their size, hummingbirds are aerial acrobats. They can rise straight up in the air like a helicopter, hover (hang in one place while flying), and turn with agility. They are also the only birds that can fly backward. Called "jewels of the air," hummingbirds sport brilliantly colored iridescent feathers in emerald green, sapphire blue, ruby red, and purple.

These tiny birds have the fastest metabolic rates—the speed at which food is digested and body wastes passed through—of all birds and mammals (except perhaps shrews). To stay alive, hummingbirds have to eat almost all the time that they are awake. They feed while hovering, using their bristle-tipped tongue to snatch insects and spiders and to slurp nectar from flowers. At night, or when the weather is too rainy or windy for them to hover and feed, hummingbirds perch and go into torpor: their body temperature drops as much as 50 degrees F and they cut their metabolic rate to a third of normal.

Sphinx moth and desert evening primrose

Sphinx moths are about the same size as hummingbirds. But unlike hummingbirds, sphinx moths' heavy bodies require four wings—two sets—to become airborne. Still, their flight is so agile that sphinx moths are often called hummingbird moths. Sphinx moths hover to feed on flower nectar, sucking through a hollow "tongue" as thick as a single human hair

and up to a foot long, which they unroll to drink and roll up when finished.

Dragonflies are hoverers too, but they don't sip nectar. They are the hawks of the insect world, zipping around in pursuit of smaller flying insects to eat. Adult dragonflies are among the largest of insects, with wingspans up to 7 inches. (But that is puny compared to their prehistoric ancestors: dragonflies with $2\frac{1}{2}$-foot wingspans!) Although their wings beat a relatively slow 30 times per second—while bees' wings, for instance, beat at 200 times per second—dragonflies can fly distances of hundreds of miles. Dragonflies are only found around water. Their larvae (young dragonflies)—stout, dark, wingless creatures—live in water.

HOW TO HOVER Many birds, such as hawks, need a strong wind in order to hover. They "tread air" by facing into the wind and beating their wings just enough to stay in place. But hummingbirds are able to hover without the wind. They beat their wings as quickly as 80 times a *second*. (The name "hummingbird" comes from the audible whir of their wings.) Huge flight muscles—equal to a third of the hummingbird's body weight—power long, narrow wings. Their stiff, broad tail works like a rudder for lightning-quick direction changes.

HOT TIP!

The Southwest is a hummingbird-watcher's paradise, boasting 15 of North America's 17 species. Feeder stations in the canyons of the Chiricahua and Huachuca mountains in southern Arizona offer the best hummingbird-watching, but look for hummingbirds around red flowers anywhere in the Southwest.

FEEDING FRENZY It may take 1,000 flowers to fuel a hummingbird for one day. If you had the metabolism of a hummingbird, you would have to eat 300 pounds of food and drink 150 gallons of water a day! How do these hovering feeders know which flowers contain sugary food? Hummingbirds literally see red. They look for red, tube-shaped flowers, but will buzz over to investigate anything red, including red hummingbird feeders or a red bandana. On the other hand, sphinx moths, flying in the dim light of evening or night, search for smells. They sniff out fragrant flowers with their antennae. Night-opening flowers are light-colored, to show up well in the dark.

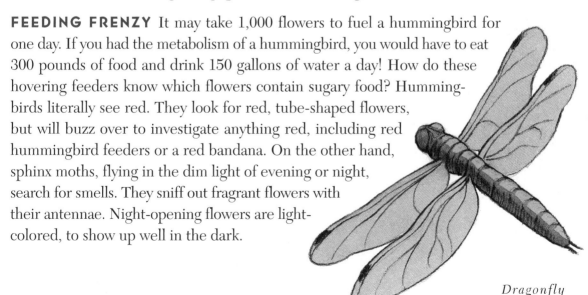

Dragonfly

GRAND CANYON, ARIZONA; NARROWS OF THE VIRGIN RIVER, UTAH; GOOSENECKS OF THE SAN JUAN, UTAH

Awwwesome Chasms

THE SOUTHWEST IS CUT BY SOME OF the world's most spectacular canyons, from Santa Elena Canyon in Big Bend National Park, Texas, where the mighty Rio Grande seems to vanish in a crack in a cliff, to North America's biggest canyon, mile-deep Grand Canyon, to the sheltered Canyon deChelly (say deSHAY), home to the long-disappeared Anasazi people.

The best place in the Southwest to go canyon hunting is the Colorado Plateau, home to the Grand Canyon. When powerful geologic forces about 65 million years ago began raising the Rocky Mountains and the many mountain ranges throughout what is now the Southwest, the thick layers of rock that make up the Colorado Plateau stayed pretty much intact, like a giant layer cake. The whole area was pushed up a mile and more above sea level. Since then, rivers and streams have eaten their way into the thick layers of sandstone, limestone, and shale of the Colorado Plateau, forming deep canyons.

HOW WATER CUTS ROCK When water runs across the ground, it picks up bits of soil, sand, pebbles, and other debris. With these "tools," water can grind away rock the way sandpaper smooths wood. Soft rock, like shale and mudstone, wears away quickly; harder rock, like granite, wears down more slowly. It takes a long time to carve a whole canyon. The Colorado River has spent about five million years on the Grand Canyon so far and continues

YOU CAN DO IT! A magical canyon hike is the Gateway to the Narrows Trail in Zion National Park, Utah. From the trailhead, hike 1 mile to the entrance to the Narrows, where the canyon walls squeeze in so tightly that there is only space for the river. To hike on, you must wade upriver. (You must also get a permit from park rangers.) Caution! Dangerous flash floods occur in the Narrows between July and early September. If you plan to hike into the Narrows, late June or late September through October are best; any month is good for the Gateway trail.

to carve away at it. To experience canyon-carving in action, watch sand move along a streambed or listen for the cracking sound boulders make as they smack into each other while rolling along a riverbed.

CANYON FACTS

- **Biggest:** The Grand Canyon in northern Arizona, over 10 miles across and 277 miles long.

- **Deepest:** The Grand Canyon, over a mile deep from the top of the North Rim to the bottom of the inner gorge. At Toroweap Point, the canyon wall drops 3,000 feet straight down to the Colorado River.

- **Narrowest:** The Narrows of the Virgin River in Zion National Park, Utah, where the canyon walls are just over 20 feet apart and 2,000 feet high!

- **Most Winding:** The Goosenecks of the San Juan River in southern Utah. Its curves loop back on each other in such tight turns that only narrow "necks" of rock now separate adjacent curves of the river channel.

OUTLAWS Just west of Canyonlands National Park in Utah, the Robbers Roost area of canyons served as the hideout for Butch Cassidy and his Wild Bunch of outlaws in the late 1800s. After robbing a bank, the Wild Bunch would lose their pursuers by riding into the maze of canyons. The area is still hard to reach, a bare wilderness of sculptured rock accessible only by rugged four-wheel-drive roads or by foot.

What's in a Name?

THE SOUTHWEST IS MULTILINGUAL: many different languages are spoken in the region. You'll hear English, of course, and Spanish, and, depending on where you are in the Southwest, you may hear one of the many different Native American lan-

NAMES ON THE LANDSCAPE

guages, like Navajo, Apache, Zuni, Hopi, Pima, O'odham, one of the Pueblo languages, or Yaqui. Often people mix two or more languages in the same sentence, such as English sprinkled with Spanish words or Zuni with some English words.

The many different kinds of people who have lived and do live in the Southwest have put names on the landscape in their own language. Thus, towns, hills, rivers, lakes, streams, mesas, and mountains in the Southwest have a variety of strange and wonderful names. For instance, El Paso, Texas ("the pass" in Spanish); Bullfrog Marina, Utah (a boat landing where bullfrogs live); and the Akimel O'odham Reservation in Arizona (home of the "running-water people" in Papago).

Places are sometimes named for an event, like Dead Horse Point, Utah, where a horse died of starvation, or Silver City, New Mexico, where silver was discovered. Places are also named for people, such as Los Lunas, named for the Luna family, early Spanish settlers of New Mexico. Places are also named for how they look, such as Mitten Butte, a mitten-shaped sandstone butte, complete with a thumb, found in Monument Valley, Arizona, or the Colorado River, which means the "colored" river in Spanish, named for the water tinged red by the sediment it carries.

Sometimes places have two or more common names because people speaking different languages each named them. For example, Shiprock, a prominent landmark in northwestern New Mexico, is also called *Tsé bit'*

YOU CAN DO IT! Look on the map and see how many names come from different languages. Besides English, Spanish is the most common language of the Southwest. Here are some common Spanish place names:

■ canyon: spelled *cañon* in Spanish. Say cahn-YONE.

■ mesa: "table" in Spanish, used for a flat-topped hill. Say MAY-suh.

■ arroyo: "gutter" in Spanish, used for a dry, eroded gulch. Say uh-RROY-oh, rolling the r's with your tongue.

■ río: means "river" in Spanish. Say REE-oh.

IT'S ALL GREEK TO ME

Scientists give animals and plants special two-part names using Latin or Greek words that can be understood by all scientists, no matter what language they speak. Scientific names look like tongue twisters, but they make sense. For example, take *Carnegia gigantea*, the saguaro cactus. *Carnegia* (say car-NAY-gee-uh) is a Greek version of the last name of Andrew Carnegie, a wealthy man who funded the expedition that first described saguaro cacti. *Gigantea* (say jiy-gan-TEE-uh) is Greek for giant, because saguaros are one of the tallest kinds of cacti in the world.

a' i or "rock with wings" (say tsuh-bit-UH-ih) in Navajo. Sometimes people didn't understand each other's languages, resulting in funny combinations, like Canyon de Chelly in northern Arizona. The Navajo word for the place, *tsegi*, means "rocky canyon." *Tsegi* sounded like "shay" (written *chelly*) to a Spaniard who didn't know Navajo. Hence, "canyon of rocky canyon"! Or Rio Grande River, which means "great river river."

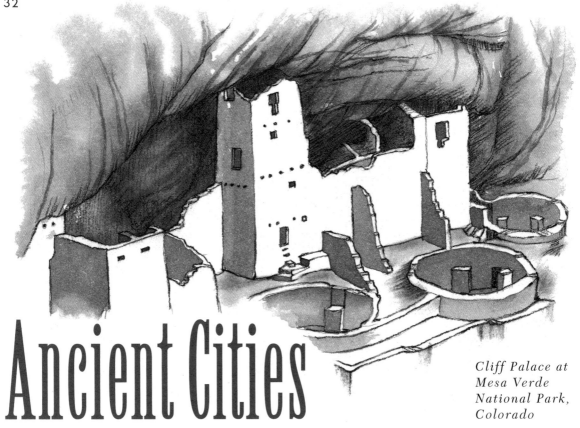

Cliff Palace at Mesa Verde National Park, Colorado

Ancient Cities

WHERE IS THE OLDEST CONTINUOUSLY OCCUPIED TOWN in the United States? Not Plymouth, Massachusetts, the landing place of the Pilgrims. Two towns in the Southwest compete for the title of oldest: Ácoma Pueblo, a village built atop a 365-foot-high mesa in western New Mexico, and old Oraibi, a Hopi village perched on Third Mesa in northern Arizona. These *pueblos,* Spanish for "towns," were founded at least 500 years before the Pilgrims landed in 1620.

PUEBLOS
CLIFF DWELLINGS

Ruins of pueblos like Ácoma and Oraibi are found throughout the Southwest. Some were built on mesa tops; others, called "cliff dwellings," were built under rock overhangs high up in cliff walls. These ancient cities were very different from our cities today. People lived in several-story-tall "apartment buildings" in small, low-ceilinged rooms, built of adobe—sun-dried brick—and stone. Instead of using stairs or elevators to reach the upper stories, people climbed outside ladders and entered through a hole in the roof. The buildings were built around plazas, open areas where people worked, children played, and town events were held. Each plaza contained at least one round, sunken room called a *kiva,* a combination community hall and church, a gathering place for social events and ceremonies. Some larger pueblos were linked by networks of stone roads. Carefully designed irrigation systems caught the sparse rainfall to water fields of corn, beans, and squash.

Many of these ancient cities stand empty today, their many-storied apartment houses partly collapsed and their plazas quiet. Nearly 700 years ago, a long drought dried up springs and streams throughout the Southwest. Crops failed and people starved. Eventually, the people abandoned the Southwest's ancient cities, moved closer to the few remaining permanent rivers and streams, and built new pueblos. Their descendants, today's Hopi, Pueblo, O'odham, Pima, and other Southwest Native Americans, live on in the new pueblos, weaving modern lives with the culture of their ancestors.

YOU CAN DO IT! To make your own tortilla chips, cut corn tortillas into eight wedge-shaped pieces. Place the pieces on a baking sheet and sprinkle them lightly with cold water, then with salt. Bake for 5 minutes in a 400 degree F oven, or until crunchy.

FROM MUD TO POT Early Southwesterners made pots with clay dug from riverbanks. After shaping the pots by hand, they decorated them with designs ranging from simple zigzags to intricate imaginary creatures, and baked them in holes dug in the ground and lined with hot rocks. Pots were often traded to traveling merchants. Archaeologists, people who study ancient cultures, can identify where the pots came from by analyzing the mineral content of the clay. Clay from different places is as unique as people's fingerprints.

CELEBRATING CORN Around 2,000 years ago, the ancient Southwesterners learned how to plant corn from people in what is now Mexico. Corn gave them a more dependable food supply than wild plants and animals. Corn is still a Southwest staple. It is eaten fresh, or dried and cooked in *posole* (say poh-SOH-lay), a kind of stew. It is ground into meal to make tortillas, piki, and other flat breads. Ground corn is also used to make a hot cereal and a hot drink. In addition to familiar yellow corn, Southwesterners grow blue, white, red, and even multicolored corn. Corn is a sacred symbol of life to many Southwesterners.

LOOK FOR:

- The Southwest's largest cliff dwelling, 200-plus-room Cliff Palace, at Mesa Verde National Park in southwestern Colorado.

- An adobe skyscraper called Casa Grande, Spanish for "big house," near Phoenix, Arizona. Its three-story-tall mud walls are 4 feet thick at the base.

- The largest known kiva, Casa Rinconada, a circular chamber 64 feet in diameter (longer than two school buses placed end to end) at the Anasazi ruins in Chaco Canyon in northwestern New Mexico. Openings in its walls line up with the rising sun at the winter solstice.

- The ruins of the Southwest's biggest city, once home to thousands of people, at Casas Grandes, Chihuahua, in northern Mexico. This sophisticated city boasted running water in stone-lined pipes.

Rock Art

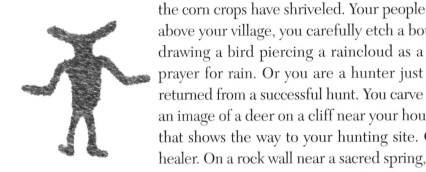

IMAGINE A LONG TIME AGO, before books or maps or writing. You are a village elder. The rains have not come this year, and the corn crops have shriveled. Your people are starving. On a ridge above your village, you carefully etch a boulder with a hard stone, drawing a bird piercing a raincloud as a prayer for rain. Or you are a hunter just returned from a successful hunt. You carve an image of a deer on a cliff near your house. Its antlers are a map that shows the way to your hunting site. Or you are a priest and healer. On a rock wall near a sacred spring, you paint huge, godlike figures with staring eyes to watch over your people.

PETROGLYPHS
PICTOGRAPHS

As long as 3,000 years ago, people who lived in the Southwest painted or chipped drawings on cliffs and rocks. Preserved by the dry climate, this rock art is a link to the past, to a history that we do not know. Rock art images vary from realistic drawings of animals like pronghorn or bats to highly abstract geometric designs. (One way to tell the age of rock art is whether the images include horses. Horses were brought to the Southwest by Spanish explorers around 400 years ago: rock art with horses is younger than 400 years old.)

YOU CAN DO IT! FINGER PAINTING. Pictograph painters ground up colored rock for pigments. They painted with their fingers, used brushes made from chewed yucca leaf tips, blew paint through hollow reeds, and scratched lines through painted areas with sticks. You can make your own pictograph on paper with nontoxic fingerpaints, your hands, brushes, and straws. Put one hand down flat on paper with your fingers spread out. Carefully suck up some paint into the tip of one end of a straw (don't get it in your mouth or swallow any!). Blow the paint around your fingers, refilling the straw as often as necessary, until you have outlined your hand with paint. Lift up your hand—you have made a pictograph! Experiment with outlining your hand with paint on a brush, and by using your fingers to paint an outline. Notice how different each outline looks.

CHIPPING ROCK Petroglyphs are often simple designs or figures. They look easy to make, but they are not. The carver uses harder rocks as hammers to chip, chisel, or scratch a design into the rock. Chipping a simple line in rock using stone tools can take hours.

Some rock art images may be prayers, others messages like "look for bighorn sheep near the spring in the next canyon." Some use the play of light and shadow to mark important dates in the yearly calendar, such as the time to prepare fields for planting.

There are two basic kinds of rock art: petroglyphs and pictographs. Petroglyphs, from the Greek *petros,* "rock," and *glyphe,* "carving," are carved or chiseled into the rock. Pictographs, from *pictor,* or "painter," and *graphein,* "to write," are paintings on rock.

All rock art is sacred. Native Americans still often worship at rock art sites. Look, but don't touch—the oil on your skin can damage rock art.

LOOK FOR:

☐ Petroglyph National Monument, the first monument established solely for rock art, just west of Albuquerque, New Mexico. Fifteen thousand petroglyphs, some prehistoric, some modern, decorate a 17-mile-long ridge.

☐ A thousand-or-more-year-old pictograph that looks like a red dragon in Black Dragon Canyon, just west of Green River, Utah.

☐ Newspaper Rock, near Monticello, Utah, named for the hundreds of petroglyphs, some 3,000 years old, some as recent as the last century, carved into its surface. Navajos call it *Tse hani,* "rock that tells a story."

☐ The "sun serpent" at Hovenweep National Monument in southwestern Colorado. Just after sunrise at summer solstice, the longest day of the year, sunlight pours through a narrow space between two boulders at just the right angle so that the light forms two serpentlike shapes crossing sun symbol petroglyphs. (Ask for directions at the Visitor Center.)

Savvy Survivors

SOME ANIMALS ARE PICKY EATERS. They specialize in one sort of food. For instance, beavers prefer aspen and cottonwood bark. One bird, the belted kingfisher, eats mostly fish. Eating just one kind of food makes hunting or foraging simpler—you need only to learn how to recognize and search for your particular food. Of course, if your food isn't available, you may starve.

COYOTES
RAVENS

Omnivores ("eaters of all"), like coyotes and ravens, don't specialize in hunting or eating any particular food. This makes them very adaptable—if one particular food isn't available, they find something else to eat. And it also means that they are good at solving problems, such as figuring out how to get new foods.

Being adaptable has helped coyotes and ravens survive the changes in the Southwest. Many wild animals are forced to flee to uninhabited areas when humans move into their territory. But not coyotes. These small wild dogs have learned how to live and hunt where people live. They den in places like abandoned cars. At night, they roam alleys and backyards in search of mice and other small animals, pet food left outside, garbage, and fruits and vegetables from gardens. Ravens, too, have adapted to people; they roost in towns, forage for spilled corn in fields, pick pecans from trees in orchards, and find tidbits in garbage dumps.

A good investigative sense has also helped coyotes and ravens survive the abuse people heap on them. For the past hundred years, trappers have shot, poisoned, and trapped hundreds of thousands of coyotes, mountain lions, wolves, eagles, bears, and other predators because they sometimes eat domestic livestock. Ravens, raccoons, and other animals that sometimes eat crops have also been shot or poisoned because they are considered "nuisance" animals. Until a century ago, the Southwest was home to grizzly bears, wolves, and jaguars. All are gone now, killed by humans. But coyotes and ravens thrive, in part because they have learned to adapt to ever-changing habitats.

HOT TIP!

Coyotes live throughout the Southwest. You are most likely to see or hear them howl at night; they are most active from dusk to dawn. Two kinds of ravens live in the Southwest: common ravens and Chihuahuan ravens. Bigger, shaggy common ravens live at higher elevations, from the foothills to the mountaintops, and are more likely to be solitary. Crow-sized Chihuahuan ravens live only in the hot desert grasslands of the very southern Southwest, and are most often found in groups.

TRICKSTER AND TROUBLEMAKER Old Man Coyote, a clever mischief-maker, is the star of many Southwest Native American stories. Coyote is always trying to trick someone else so that he doesn't have to work so hard, or to fool people into giving him more than his share. He often succeeds for a while, but in the end, the joke is usually on Coyote. These stories entertain and teach people how to behave through Coyote's many misadventures.

HOWLING HELLOS Like all dogs, coyotes "talk" to one another by barking, whining, yipping, howling, and also by wagging their tails, curling their lips, play fighting, and marking scent posts. But coyotes, called "song dogs" in some Native American languages, have a bigger vocabulary than any other domestic or wild dogs. Coyotes are very social, and their howling talk helps them maintain their family ties. The most familiar coyote song—the *yip! yip! yip! oo-oo-oow!* group howl—brings group members back together before or after hunting.

Desert Rats

ROADRUNNERS AND KANGAROO RATS are so well adapted to the extreme conditions of desert life that they have become symbols of the Southwest.

ROADRUNNERS
KANGAROO RATS

Roadrunners seem comical. They are long-legged and large, stretching almost 2 feet from the tip of their oversized beak to the end of their long tail. Their feathers are speckled black and white, and bare skin around their eyes is cartoonishly colored bright red and blue. They constantly raise and lower the crest atop their head like a signal flag.

Unlike many desert animals, which take refuge from the extremes of desert weather, roadrunners are active in both the hottest and coldest months. In summer, they compress their feathers to retain less heat and take to the shade on the hottest days. In winter, roadrunners save energy by using the sun's heat to warm themselves. They turn their back toward the sun, and raise the feathers on their crest and back to expose their jet black skin. The black skin absorbs heat quickly, warming the chilled bird. Like many desert dwellers, roadrunners adjust their brood size to the rains. In rainy years when food is plentiful, they may lay a dozen eggs. But if the rains don't come and food is scarce, they don't lay any eggs.

True to their name, roadrunners would rather run than fly. They hunt on the run, sprinting as fast as 15 miles an hour to catch insects, lizards, scorpions, birds, and other small animals. If you see a roadrunner with something dangling from its beak, look closer. When they catch a lizard or snake too big to swallow whole, the excess dangles from their beak until they have room to swallow it!

Kangaroo rats are not kangaroos, nor are they rats. These mouse-sized rodents get their name

HOT TIP!

Look for roadrunners along roadsides in the deserts of the southern Southwest, such as at Big Bend National Park in Texas, and Saguaro National Park in Arizona.

Kangaroo rat homes are found throughout the lower elevations of the Southwest. Look for bare mounds of earth as much as 6 feet across, with several entrances, each about the diameter of a soda can. Abandoned burrows house other animals, including scorpions and rattlesnakes, so don't stick your hand into a burrow!

from their huge hind legs, which they use to spring up to 10 feet, their hopping gait, and their long tail. Kangaroo rats have a breakaway tail, like many lizards; if grabbed by a predator, the tail breaks off and the kangaroo rat escapes. (The tail doesn't grow back, though.)

Kangaroo rats can survive without ever drinking water. They get what little water they need from digesting their food, mainly plant seeds, and by conserving moisture. They are nocturnal, avoiding the heat and sun. Kangaroo rats spend the days in their burrows, plugging the burrow entrances to keep the inside air cool and moist. They even save water by concentrating their body wastes—their droppings contain half the water of human waste.

FAT CHEEKS Kangaroo rats and their cousins, pocket mice, have fur-lined pockets in their cheeks—outside their mouth—where they stash seeds. After they fill their cheek pouches, these small rodents dash back to the safety of their burrow to eat. Kangaroo rat cheek pouches stuffed full can hold up to 900 small seeds.

Kangaroo rat

WHO IS THE FASTEST? Roadrunners have a reputation for speed, but they are not the fastest animals in the Southwest. Pronghorn, clocked at over 50 miles an hour for short bursts, may be the fastest on land. Mountain lions come close to pronghorns' speed, and jackrabbits have been clocked at 30 miles an hour. Peregrine falcons are the speedsters of the air. They can dive at speeds of up to 200 miles an hour!

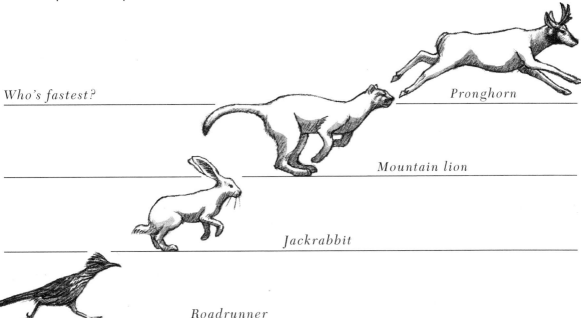

Who's fastest?

Pronghorn

Mountain lion

Jackrabbit

Roadrunner

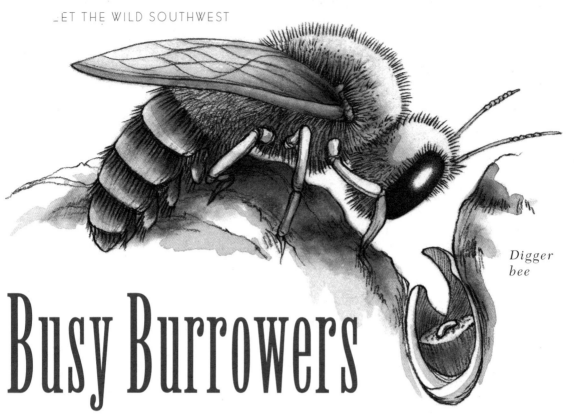

*Digger
bee*

Busy Burrowers

HAVE YOU EVER EXPLORED A CAVE? No matter what the conditions above-ground, inside a cave the air remains a constant temperature—never too hot, never too cold, never too dry. No wonder then, that so many animals in the Southwest—

PRAIRIE DOGS
DIGGER BEES

from ants to black bears, spadefoot toads to rattlesnakes—spend part of their lives underground.

Prairie dogs are one of the Southwest's master burrowers. These chubby, foot-long relatives of ground squirrels use short, muscular forelegs and stout claws to excavate networks of tunnels up to 15 feet long, as deep as 6 feet beneath the ground. They pile the scooped-out earth around the burrow entrance, building a perfect lookout post; it also keeps water from pouring into the burrow. Prairie dogs air out their underground houses by building one entrance higher than the others, which pulls fresh air through their burrow.

Prairie dogs spend their days above ground near their burrow entrances, eating grass, grooming one another, and watching for predators like badgers, hawks, eagles, coyotes, or bobcats. When one prairie dog sounds the danger alert with a sharp bark, all dive for their holes.

Billions of prairie dogs once lived in sprawling colonies throughout the dry grass-lands of western North America, from Alberta, Canada, to Mexico. One colony in Texas covered 25,000 square miles—the size of the state of West Virginia—and housed 400 million prairie dogs! Prairie dogs are no longer so common—the Utah prairie dog is endangered—because people killed them off, thinking to improve cattle grazing. Actually, prairie dog tunneling enriches the soil; their grazing stimulates new grass growth.

Another master burrower is the Sonoran Desert digger bee. These residents of the desert of southern and central Arizona and northern Mexico spend most of their short lives about 6 inches underground. Just before the palo verde trees bloom, male digger bees push their way to the earth's surface, then cruise close to the ground in search of still-buried females, which they locate by smell. After mating, a female digs a brood chamber in the desert soil, stocks the hole with palo verde flower nectar and pollen, then lays an egg in it. After she plugs that hole, she digs another, and another, digging as many brood chambers as she can while the palo verde trees are in bloom. Her young spend the next 11 months underground, emerging just in time for palo verde blossoming. And the cycle repeats.

UNDERGROUND CITIES Each prairie dog colony is divided into half-acre neighborhoods called coteries, inhabited by one male, several females, and the young of the year. Coterie members greet each other by "kissing," gently touching noses and lips. Prairie dogs talk with sounds and body language. Whitetail prairie dogs have developed such a specific language that they can warn others of danger, and even describe the kind of predator that is approaching.

HOUSEHOLD PESTS Fleas, mites, lice, and other tiny grazers move into burrows to feed on the occupants' droppings, skin flakes, and discarded food. Eventually these pests force the occupants to abandon the burrow. After the burrow is empty, the pests die out, and other animals move in.

Prairie dog

HOT TIP!

Who lives in all those holes in the ground? Lizards, spiders, and mice dig holes no larger than the diameter of a very fat crayon (about 1 1/2 inches). Spider holes are usually lined or covered with whitish strands of spider silk. Ground squirrels or pocket gophers dig holes about the diameter of a soda pop can. Ground squirrels live in colonies (look for several holes); pocket gophers don't. Rock squirrels and skunks dig holes the diameter of a coffee can (4 to 5 inches). Sniff the hole—you'll know if it belongs to a skunk! Holes a foot or more across may belong to kit foxes, badgers, or coyotes. Kit fox holes are taller than wide, badger holes wider than tall. Coyote holes are almost big enough to crawl into—but don't do it. Snakes, burrowing owls, and other desert animals that can't dig their own holes move into abandoned burrows.

Creepy Crawlies

CENTIPEDES AND MILLIPEDES ARE BOTH CREEPY, crawling creatures with many legs. But they are very different. Centipedes are meat eaters that kill their prey by squeezing it with poison-containing pincers on their first pair of legs. Milli-

CENTIPEDES
MILLIPEDES

pedes graze on plant material and repel predators (like centipedes) by expelling a smelly vapor from their repugnatorial gland, an organ at the end of their body. Both have long, many-segmented bodies. Centipedes have flattened bodies, with one pair of legs per body segment. Milli-pedes' bodies are rounded and wormlike, with two pairs of legs per body segment.

Centipedes were named in the mistaken belief that they possessed 100 feet (in Latin, *centi* means "one hundred," *pede* means "feet"). Actually, they may have as few as 30 feet or as many as 362. Despite their many feet and legs, centipedes move quickly and gracefully. Some centipedes can scurry along at speeds of over a foot per second. Many centipedes have detachable legs. If a predator grabs a centipede leg, the leg breaks off and continues to wiggle, distracting the attacker. A new leg eventually grows to replace the missing one.

Centipedes are ferocious hunters, despite poor sight. They hunt at night, using antennae and sensitive hairs on their feet to smell and see prey. Once a centipede locates a tasty animal, it subdues the prey with its poisonous pin-cers, then eats it. Smaller centipedes eat insects and spi-ders, including cockroaches and houseflies, so they make good housemates for humans. But larger centipedes, like the 9-inch-long giant desert centipede found in the deserts of the southern Southwest and northern Mexico, don't

HOT TIP!

Look for centipedes and millipedes in the lower elevations of the southern Southwest on summer nights, especially after rains. They often shelter under rocks, branches, or pieces of bark. Look cautiously—scorpions hide in the same places.

Millipede

DANGER!

Centipedes deliver a painful pinch, including a dose of poison. You won't die from the bite of any Southwestern centipede, but a bad bite can hurt as much as a bee sting. The larger the centipede, the more dangerous the bite. Small centipedes are harmless, but people have died from the bites of foot-long tropical centipedes.

make good housemates—they pack a painful bite. Giant desert centipedes, North America's largest, dine on lizards, small snakes, and mice. A surprised scientist once watched a 4-inch giant desert centipede kill and carry off a 10-inch snake!

Unlike speedy centipedes, millipedes move slowly. They graze on dead leaves, the bark of shrubs, and other plant litter. In dry climates, dead plants don't decay quickly; millipedes and other creatures help break down and recycle plant material. Millipedes escape hot and dry desert conditions by spending as much as three-quarters of the year underground in abandoned burrows or in the nests of other animals (including harvester ants), emerging above ground after summer rains.

Most predators are repelled by a millipede's smelly vapor. But glowworms—firefly larvae—eat millipedes, perhaps because, unable to smell, they are not bothered by the stink.

TOO MANY LEGS Centipedes and millipedes look like insects, but they are not. They have too many legs. Centipedes never have fewer than 30 legs, millipedes no fewer than 32 legs. True insects, however, have only six legs. (Spiders have eight.) But centipedes, millipedes, insects, and spiders are all arthropods: critters with external, jointed skeletons.

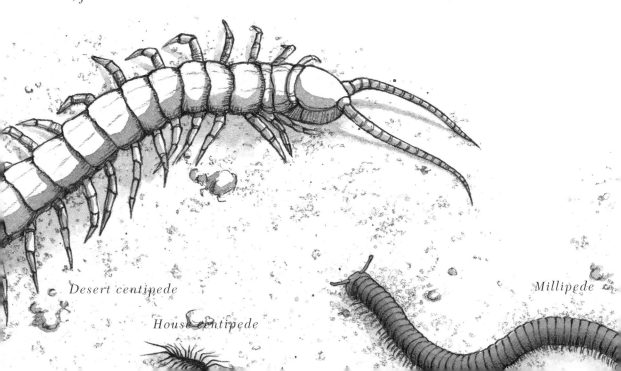

Desert centipede

Millipede

House centipede

Plant Poisons

WHAT ARE THE MOST DANGEROUS THINGS
you might encounter in the Southwest?
Rattlesnakes? Scorpions? Heatstroke or dehydra-

SACRED DATURA
WATER HEMLOCK
FLY AGARIC

tion? These can kill you, but
some of the deadliest substances in the world are
found in the Southwest: in

two plants, sacred datura and water hemlock, and a
mushroom called fly agaric.

Poisonous substances protect plants and fungi
from being munched by grazing animals. If a
mouthful makes a grazer sick, the animal learns to
avoid that plant. Sometimes only one part of the
plant is poisonous. Rhubarb leaves, for example, are
poisonous to humans, but the cooked stems are delicious.

Sacred datura, or *toloache* (say toe-low-AH-chay) in Spanish, is beautiful to look at
and deadly poisonous. Each part of the plant contains poisonous alkaloids, chemicals
that affect your brain. Eating even small amounts of datura can cause you to hallucinate,
go blind, dehydrate, and die. (Try not to touch the plant—the poison can get on your

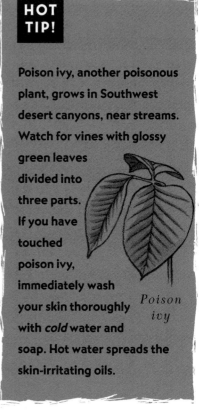

HOT TIP!

Poison ivy, another poisonous
plant, grows in Southwest
desert canyons, near streams.
Watch for vines with glossy
green leaves
divided into
three parts.
If you have
touched
poison ivy,
immediately wash
your skin thoroughly
with *cold* water and
soap. Hot water spreads the
skin-irritating oils.

Poison ivy

Sacred datura

hands and eventually in your mouth.) But datura is one of the desert's most stunning and easily recognized wildflowers. Its huge, trumpet-shaped blossoms shimmer ghostly white in the summer moonlight and smell like sweet lemons. Zuni Pueblo stories say that sacred datura sprouts in memory of two children who were banished by the gods for telling religious secrets. Sacred datura is common throughout the Southwest, from the deserts to the piñon-juniper woodlands, and often grows on roadsides.

Water hemlock, another deadly poisonous plant, is less common than sacred datura. In the Southwest, it flourishes only near water high in the mountains, above 6,000 feet elevation. This relative of carrots, celery, and caraway grows 2 to 4 feet tall and looks like Queen Anne's lace, with lacy clusters of tiny white flowers atop the plant. Water hemlock is so poisonous that you could die after eating a piece the size of a marble.

Fly agaric, an amanita mushroom with a pretty red or orange cap dotted with white bumps, is so deadly that eating just one cap can cause you to bleed to death internally. Fly agaric, or fly fungus, was mashed into milk and used as a pesticide in some parts of Europe. This deadly mushroom grows in pine and spruce-fir forests in the mountains of the Southwest and sprouts after summer rains.

Warning! Fly agaric looks like some edible mushrooms. Don't touch, pick, or eat anything that you can't *positively* identify.

Fly agaric

DEATH IN THE DESERT In June 1994, three teenagers from El Paso, Texas, decided to try to get high on sacred datura. They brewed a tea from its leaves and drank it at a party in the desert. Two of the teens died the next day of heatstroke and dehydration caused by the datura. The third staggered home a day later, delirious, his tongue stuck to the roof of his mouth.

YOU CAN DO IT! One way you can identify mushrooms is by making spore prints. A mushroom produces millions of tiny spores—its "seeds"—between its gills. Different species' spores are different colors. To make spore prints, you need mushrooms with gills, pieces of white paper and black paper, and bowls to cover the mushroom caps. Carefully take the stalk off a mushroom and place the cap, gills down, on a piece of either white or black paper—white if the spores look dark, black if the spores look light. Cover the mushroom cap with a bowl and leave it overnight. Take the bowl off and remove the cap to see the "print" made by the spores. *Mushrooms and Truffles of the Southwest* (see *Wild Books* at the back of this book) can help you identify the mushrooms you made spore prints of.

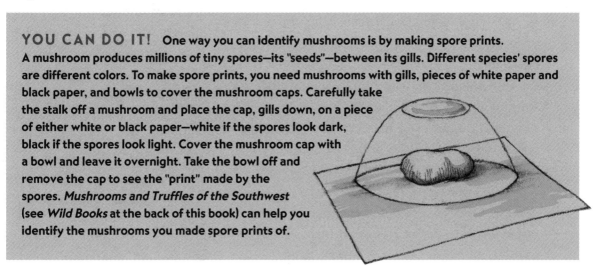

Look-Alikes

IMAGINE THAT YOU ARE A TREE. Your trunk is white and straight. Your leaves are small and rounded and rustle pleasantly in the breeze. Around you is a crowd of trees that look almost exactly like you. You are all connected by your roots, sharing food and water. Your genes, the biological codes that control you, are identical to those of the other trees. Who are you? Are you an individual or not?

ASPEN
GAMBEL OAK

You are an aspen tree, part of a superorganism, a living being made up of many identical, connected individuals. Aspen clones, groves of identical trees, all sprout from the same root system and are part of the same plant. A clone can include a few identical trees or many thousands. The aspen clones that grow on the mesas of western Colorado contain millions of trees each and may be the largest organisms in the world.

One clone, or grove, of aspens may look very different from another clone, because they are different organisms. But the trees within each clone are nearly identical. All are about the same height. Their bark is the same color, either white or olive green, and either smooth or marked with black bumps. All grow either straight as an arrow shaft or crooked as a lightning bolt. In spring and fall, it is easy to tell adjacent clones apart. The trees in one clone all leaf out at the same time, and all turn gold and fall at the same time. But different clones may be on very different schedules, depending on water and temperature conditions, and so they leaf out or turn gold weeks apart.

HOT TIP!

Look for aspen at the Southwest's highest elevations, from around 7,500 to 11,000 feet. You can spot aspens: their heart-shaped leaves "quake" (flutter back and forth in the breeze) because they have flat stems turned 180 degrees to the leaf's surface. Good places for viewing aspens' fall gold include Bryce Canyon and Zion national parks in southern Utah; the North Rim of the Grand Canyon and the San Francisco Peaks in northern Arizona; southern Colorado's Mesa Verde National Park; northern New Mexico's upper Rio Grande Valley; and the Guadalupe Mountains in west Texas.

Growing in clones may be the aspen's way of adapting to frequent forest fires. Ground fires caused by lightning are a natural part of many western forests. Fire sweeps through the forest, clearing out the underbrush and fertilizing the ground. The sprawling roots of an aspen clone can quickly send up new sprouts, producing an "instant forest" to recolonize a burned area.

Gambel oak leaves and acorns

Gambel oak, the only Southwest oak with classically oak-shaped, deciduous leaves (leaves that fall off in winter), also forms clones in some parts of its range. In northern Mexico and the southern Southwest, it doesn't form clones; here Gambel oak grows as small, widely scattered trees. But farther north on the Colorado Plateau and the southern Rocky Mountains, Gambel oak grows as clones of dense, head-high shrubs. These nearly impenetrable thickets are called chaparral, from the Spanish word *chaps* (say shaps), the leather leg coverings that protect horse riders' legs from the thick brush. These Gambel oak clones grow in places too cold for Gambel oak acorns to sprout today. Scientists think these clones may have begun thousands of years ago, sprouted from acorns when the climate was warmer.

SISTERS Some animals also clone themselves. Certain species of whiptail lizards—small, hyperactive, long-tailed lizards of the southern Southwest—are unisexual, all female. There are no males. The females lay self-fertilized eggs just like all lizards, but the eggs hatch into exact replicas of their mother.

Whiptail lizard

FOOD FOR ALL Aspen and Gambel oak are wildlife snack bars. Deer, elk, and moose browse aspen bark and twigs. Aphids suck the sap of tender shoots, and the clear tracks of leaf miners, tiny insects that eat leaf cells, scrawl across the leaves they "mine." In winter, grouse and quail feed on aspen buds. Beaver cut and store aspen logs in their ponds for food. Aspen bark contains salicin, the original aspirin.

The fatty and nutritious acorns produced by Gambel oak are gobbled up by birds such as wild turkeys and acorn woodpeckers, as well as animals from acorn borers to peccaries and bears. People grind the acorns into meal to make mush and breads, and to thicken soups.

Canyon wren

Desert Voices

CANYON WRENS
CACTUS WRENS
NORTHERN MOCKINGBIRDS

BIRD SOUNDS ANNOUNCE THE SEASONS in the Southwest: doves' low cooing begins summer mornings; ravens' croaking heralds autumn; spring, mating season, is an explosion of song. But one of the most hauntingly beautiful of Southwest birdsongs is the canyon wren's flutelike trill, which echoes almost year-round.

Canyon wrens are small birds, just 4½ inches long from their sharp beak to short tail, a bit longer than a cassette tape. But canyon wrens have big voices. Their distinctive songs ripple down the scale, filling the air of canyons and rocky mountainsides with silvery notes. The songs are both romantic and practical: they announce a male canyon wren's territory and help him attract a mate. Canyon wrens sing even in the hottest hours of the day, when other birds are silent.

The Southwest's largest wrens, 8-inch-long cactus wrens, don't sing like canyon wrens, but their voices are just as distinctive. These big, speckled brown-and-white wrens are the desert's noisy fussbudgets. Their squawking chatter and explosive, low *chug-chug-chug-chug* can be heard wherever cacti and other spiny shrubs grow. Cactus wrens get their name because they nest and roost in the protective spiny armor of shrubby cacti, yucca, and mesquite trees. They build many large nests, bulky domes of grass and twigs that protect them from the harsh climate. These master builders take advantage of solar energy by orienting the openings of their

HOT TIP!

You are more likely to hear a canyon wren than see one. Listen for them—especially in summer—in canyons or on rocky slopes throughout the Southwest, including Zion and Canyonlands national parks in southern Utah. When you hear a flutelike solo, scan the rocks for a small rust brown bird with a bright white bib and a thin, slightly curved beak.

spring nests south to catch the warm spring sun. Summer nest openings are turned away from the south, to keep cool.

Northern mockingbirds, the Southwest's vocal mimics, are robin-sized, slender, and colored gray and white. They often flick their long tails up and down. Male mockingbirds compose long, bubbling songs that can last hours, using sounds that they imitate from their surroundings. They borrow and improvise on other birds' songs, animal noises, and even mechanical noises like sirens, squeaky doors, and car alarms. A male mockingbird can memorize and use 50 or more songs. His songs are musical advertisements used to broadcast his territory, help attract mates, and discourage competitors. Unmated males often sing all night long.

WHY DO BIRDS SING? Birdsongs serve as vocal announcements. In most species, only the males sing. (But both females and males "talk" with short calls and other sounds.) Songs identify the singer—"I am a warbling vireo." Songs attract the attention of passing females—"Come check me out. I'd make a good mate." Songs also defend the singer's territory from other males—"Stay away!" Songs can be complicated, like the orations of mockingbirds or the musical whistles, warbles, and trills of orioles. Or they can be simple, like the repeated loud whistles of red-winged blackbirds.

YOU CAN DO IT! During spring and summer, listen for mockingbirds' songs in early morning or late evening in the Southwest's deserts and lower elevations. In towns, mockingbirds often perch on television antennae, utility poles, and roof peaks. When you hear a long, bubbling song containing many different sounds, listen carefully and you may be able to identify the borrowed sounds, from a robin's *cheerio . . . cheerio* call to a dog's barking.

Splendid Soarers

Turkey vulture

IF YOU LOOK UP INTO THE SKY on a sunny day, you are likely to see a large bird soaring in wide circles somewhere overhead. Soaring birds, like eagles, vultures, and buteos (big soaring hawks), hunt for food from high in the air, and save energy by hitching rides on thermals, rising bubbles of hot air. With their long, wide wings outstretched and tails fanned, these birds glide with ease.

GOLDEN EAGLES VULTURES BUTEOS

The biggest soaring birds now living year-round in the Southwest are golden eagles. Adult golden eagles stand about 3 feet high; their enormous wings stretch up to 7 1/2 feet from tip to tip. These days, golden eagles are protected. But these majestic birds nearly disappeared from the Southwest after more than 20,000 were killed between 1940 and 1962 for supposedly preying on young livestock. Actually, golden eagles rarely attack large mammals. Rabbits, ground squirrels, and marmots are their most common food. Golden eagles are sacred to many Native American cultures, and their long, brown wing feathers are used for ceremonial costumes.

Vultures, black soaring birds with featherless heads, are clumsy and slow on land, but are built for

HOT TIP!

Look for soaring birds on sunny afternoons. The thermals that they ride develop best over open country. Golden eagles are very big and dark brown all over, with beautiful gold front edges on their wings. They are usually solitary. Turkey vultures soar with their wings held in a deep V. Adult turkey vultures' heads are dull red, but the color isn't always visible. Black vultures hold their wings stiffly outstretched, and sport white patches at the base of their outermost wing feathers. Red-tailed hawks are easily recognized by their bright rust red tails.

the air. These homely birds can glide gracefully for hours without ever beating their wings and can even stay aloft in nearly still air. Vultures are often feared because they eat carrion (rotting animal bodies). But vultures play an important role in Southwest ecosystems: they dispose of potential sources of disease and recycle the nutrients contained in the carcasses. And they are well adapted to the role. Their unfeathered heads are easy to clean of rotten meat and potential pests. Special immune systems protect them from organisms that cause disease. They soar high in the air to scan for carrion. The record for highest bird flight in the Southwest probably goes to vultures, which climb as high as 10,000 feet in the air.

Two kinds of vultures live in the Southwest, and both roost—perch at night—in groups. Larger turkey vultures are found in open country throughout the region. Black vultures live only in the southernmost areas of the Southwest.

Many kinds of buteos (large, soaring hawks) live in the Southwest, including North America's most common and widespread soaring hawk, the red-tailed hawk. Two Southwest buteos may soar with flocks of vultures for "camouflage" when they hunt. Since vultures eat only dead animals, prey animals that might dive for cover at the sight of a hawk do not hide when they spot vultures passing overhead. Common black hawks soar with—and look like—black vultures, and zone-tailed hawks mimic turkey vultures.

SOARING GIANTS. The California condor, a huge vulture that stands 4 feet tall, with wings stretching to 9½ feet wide, was once the biggest soaring bird in the Southwest. Today only a few California condors survive, living in the mountains of southern California and in zoos. Biologists hope that by breeding condors in captivity, their numbers will increase, and someday these huge birds can soar again above the Southwest's wild spaces.

YOU CAN DO IT! You can make bird "scarehawks" for your windows and glass doors by enlarging the silhouettes shown on this page with a photocopier. Trace the outlines of the enlarged silhouettes onto black construction paper. Cut out the construction paper "scarehawks" and tape them up to keep birds from flying into the glass.

Supersonic Flyers

White-throated swifts

FALCONS
WHITE-THROATED SWIFTS

THE FASTEST BIRD IN THE SOUTHWEST is probably a peregrine falcon, which can dive earthward in pursuit of dinner at speeds of 100 to 200 miles an hour. For their size, diving falcons fly much faster than the fastest jets.

Falcons are hawks with boomerang-shaped, swept-back wings designed for quick maneuvering and breathtaking dives. Other hawks are designed for different kinds of flight. Buteos have long, wide wings and short tails for the most efficient soaring. Accipiters, or bird hawks, have long tails for quick maneuvering and short, wide wings to allow them to soar.

Falcons hunt by diving on their prey so fast that they kill it on impact. Five kinds of falcons live in the Southwest. Peregrine falcons, the speedsters of the group, were once found throughout North America, but are now endangered because of pesticide poisoning, habitat destruction, and illegal capture for falconry (the sport of hunting using hawks). To restore their numbers, peregrine falcons are being introduced in cities across the country. They nest on skyscrapers (similar to the cliff faces of their wild habitat) and dine on city pigeons, thus helping to control pigeon populations. The easiest falcons to find are kestrels, robin-sized hawks that often hover over roadsides, hunting grasshoppers and mice.

White-throated swifts, small, cigar-shaped birds with curved-back wings, fly nearly as fast as peregrine falcons. Although they normally fly at more moderate speeds of 60 to 100 miles per hour, they can accelerate fast enough to outfly the falcons. (Another species of swift has been clocked flying at 219 miles per hour!) Swifts fly as high as thousands of feet up in the air, and they zip and turn on a dime.

The white-throated swift's common name comes from the **V**-shaped white bib like a tuxedo shirtfront on its black body. Its scientific name, *Aeronautes,* means "sailor of the air" in Greek, a perfect description for birds that accomplish many of the activities of everyday life—feeding, bathing, drinking, gathering nesting material, having sex, and even napping—in flight. Swifts zoom through the air with mouth opened wide, scooping in airborne insect meals of flies, beetles, wasps, and bees, and even spiders.

BIRDS BEFORE PLANES When engineers began designing planes, they studied birds. The engineers looked at the sleek, aerodynamic body shapes of falcons and swifts, their swept-back wings and smooth plumage, for clues to making a faster airplane—the jet. Airplane framework, hollow to save weight but strong and flexible, imitates the skeletons of hawks and other large flying birds. Bird skeletons start out solid, but as birds grow, their bones are invaded by sacs attached to their lungs. The sacs grow from the lungs like tentacles and excrete a chemical that hollows out the bone cores.

FALCONRY

For thousands of years people have trained falcons to hunt and bring back their prey, such as rabbits and pigeons, for people to eat. A falconer trains a young bird to fly from a gloved hand, to return to the trainer's glove on command, and to surrender its kill. Peregrine falcons were once the most popular species for falconry. These days, falconers are not allowed to take peregrine falcons and other endangered hawks from the wild. In fact, falconers have helped in the effort to restore peregrine falcon populations. Unfortunately, endangered falcons are still sometimes stolen from the wild and sold to avid falconers, who will pay as much as $100,000 for a rare falcon.

HOT TIP!

Listen for white-throated swifts' high-pitched, chattering voices around cliffs throughout the Southwest in summer, especially near rivers and streams. (They winter in southern Mexico and Central America.) The canyons and mountains of Big Bend National Park in Texas may be the best place to find peregrine falcons in the Southwest.

Peregrine falcon

Foreigners

WHEN YOU THINK OF THE SOUTHWEST, what do you see? Rolling tumble-weeds? Cowboys driving dusty herds of cattle? A grizzled prospector trailed by his faith-ful burro? All of these images, common on television and in movies, star "foreigners" or introduced species—animals and plants that are not native to the Southwest.

Such foreigners have drastically affected the South-west landscape. Before Spanish explorers rode into the Southwest in the early 1500s, there were no horses, cows, burros, or domestic sheep and goats in the region. Instead, herds of bison, elk, deer, pronghorn, and bighorn sheep roamed the open country of the Southwest, from desert to mountaintop.

COWS, SHEEP
HORSES, BURROS
TUMBLEWEED
SALTCEDAR

After the Spaniards introduced domestic livestock, herds of foreign grazers rapidly multiplied. Eventually, too many hungry mouths competing for the same grass caused serious overgrazing. Once-fertile grasslands and desert shrublands were eaten bare. Rain falling on now-bare soils poured off in muddy torrents instead of sinking in to recharge the life-giving waters of springs, streams, and marshes. Water flooding off the newly bared landscape gouged steep-walled gullies, or arroyos, dry riverbeds where streams had flowed. Deer and elk became nearly extinct.

Today, thanks to habitat restoration, populations of deer and elk have recovered. But herds of cattle graze where bison once roamed, and desert pronghorn are still scarce. Many people think that overgrazing by domestic livestock is still degrading the

Southwest's dry grasslands and shrublands. Feral—escaped and become wild—livestock cause problems too. A herd of feral horses living on White Sands Missile Range in southern New Mexico so overgrazed their desert home that 122 horses died of starvation one recent summer.

Foreign plants have caused problems too. Tumbleweed, a spiny, globe-shaped plant that breaks off and rolls with the winds, hitchhiked to North America with crop seeds brought from Russia in the late 1800s. It found conditions favorable, and within 20 years, tumbleweed had rolled its way across the West and Southwest, springing up on abandoned fields, roadsides, and overgrazed land throughout the region. Its spiny branches spoiled hay, fouled farm machinery, and crowded out native plants. Tumbleweed is prolific: in a few months, a single tumbleweed seed can produce a plant up to 6 feet high and 15 feet across that contains 200,000 or more seeds. Ironically, this invader has become so common that tumbleweed is associated with popular images of the West.

Saltcedar, or tamarisk, a small tree with tiny, salty leaves and sweet-smelling clusters of pink flowers, is another troublesome foreigner. Introduced in the United States around the turn of the century for erosion control, windbreaks, and its pretty flowers, saltcedar has succeeded all too well. Dense thickets of saltcedar now line desert rivers and streams, crowding out the native plants and sucking up groundwater with deep roots.

WHO IS A "NATIVE" HERE? People probably didn't arrive in the Southwest until climates warmed after the last glacial age, around 15,000 years ago. These early hunters migrated here from the overcrowded and overhunted plains of Siberia. Over time, other groups of people moved in, some from the south, others from the north, each grabbing territory from the current residents. In the 1500s, the Spaniards, the first Europeans to arrive in the Southwest, claimed the country for themselves, ignoring the thousands of resident Indians. Then came the Americans, who "won" much of the Southwest from Mexico in 1846. Who are the foreigners here?

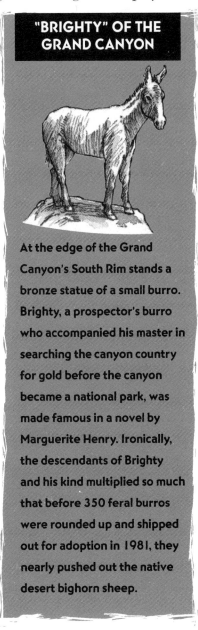

"BRIGHTY" OF THE GRAND CANYON

At the edge of the Grand Canyon's South Rim stands a bronze statue of a small burro. Brighty, a prospector's burro who accompanied his master in searching the canyon country for gold before the canyon became a national park, was made famous in a novel by Marguerite Henry. Ironically, the descendants of Brighty and his kind multiplied so much that before 350 feral burros were rounded up and shipped out for adoption in 1981, they nearly pushed out the native desert bighorn sheep.

Hungry Hordes

Mormon cricket

RAINS BRING THE DESERT TO LIFE. Plants sprout, covering formerly bare soil. Insects of all sorts hatch, baby lizards scurry everywhere, baby animals abound. In fact, the numbers of some kinds of desert animals, like grasshoppers and quail, are so closely tied to the rains that their populations vary widely from one year to the next, depending on how much rain falls.

GRASSHOPPERS
QUAIL

Hundreds of kinds of grasshoppers live throughout the Southwest. These insects can hop great distances on their long back legs and have powerful jaws for devouring plants. Grasshoppers hatch by the billions in years of abundant rains. Their main sources of food are annuals—plants that grow, bloom, make seeds, and die all in one year. Annual plants grow only when the soil is moist. In dry years, annuals don't sprout, and grasshoppers don't survive. In rainy years, annuals sprout abundantly, providing plenty of food for hatching grasshoppers. (See *Sudden Surprises*, page 84.)

Grasshoppers, in turn, are high-protein meals for many bigger animals. Birds such as kestrels, small falcons, and cactus wrens feed grasshoppers to their young. Kit foxes and coyotes pounce on grasshoppers and devour them.

You have to look carefully to find some grasshoppers. Many are camouflaged, colored, and even shaped to blend into their habitat. One tiny grasshopper species lives only on creosote bush, an olive green shrub that grows nearly everywhere in the hot deserts of the southern Southwest. Females resemble the blackish old creosote stems; males look like olive green leaf clusters. Another desert grasshopper that lives on the ground looks just like a small, stout pebble—except when it hops! (Neither of these grasshoppers has a common name. There are so many kinds of insects that most don't have common names.)

Quail are chunky, short-legged birds with nodding head plumes and spotted or streaky plumage. They run across the ground like small wind-up toys. Like grasshoppers, quail populations also vary each year depending on the amount of

HOT TIP!

Grasshoppers are common in late summer and fall throughout the Southwest, especially in deserts and grasslands. Listen for the *scritch . . . scritch* noises of their jaws rasping together as they devour plants. Listen for quail in the cooler mornings and evenings. In winter, flocks of quail gather around water holes, "talking" to one another with soft whistles and plinking calls.

rain. Some years, hordes of baby quail hatch; other years, it is hard to find even one.

Quail are very social and talkative birds. They communicate with the other members of their flock with loud whistles, soft clucks, and plinking sounds. Quail live in smaller family-group flocks during spring and summer and congregate in flocks of several hundred during the winter. When disturbed, quail run for cover, darting in different directions. If pursued, they explode into flight. The racket of their wings and the plump bodies hurtling in different directions confuses coyotes and other predators, allowing the quail time to escape. Quail chicks hatch ready to run, fully feathered, and eyes open.

A PLAGUE OF LOCUSTS In 1848, hordes of locusts—big, dark brown or blue-black grasshoppers that walk rather than fly—hatched in Utah. The ravenous grasshoppers began to eat all of the plants in their path, including the crops planted by Mormon settlers, threatening the people with starvation. The crops were saved by flocks of migrating gulls, which ate the insects. In 1913, the grateful Mormons erected a gull statue in Temple Square in Salt Lake City. These insects are called Mormon crickets.

MYSTERIOUS BIRTH CONTROL For years, scientists were puzzled by the quail's seeming ability to forecast how dry or wet a year would be. In a dry year, quail lay few or no eggs, "knowing" that there won't be food for their young. In a wet year, however, they lay several dozen eggs. How do quail know how many eggs to lay? The mystery was solved when scientists discovered that in dry years, when there is less food available, quail graze heavily on locoweeds, plants that contain toxic substances, causing the quail eggs to be aborted.

Gambel's quail

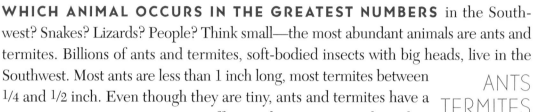

Mighty Mites

WHICH ANIMAL OCCURS IN THE GREATEST NUMBERS in the Southwest? Snakes? Lizards? People? Think small—the most abundant animals are ants and termites. Billions of ants and termites, soft-bodied insects with big heads, live in the Southwest. Most ants are less than 1 inch long, most termites between 1/4 and 1/2 inch. Even though they are tiny, ants and termites have a giant effect on the ecosystems where they live. (An ecosystem, from the Greek word *ecos*, "home," is the combination of animals, plants, and their environment.)

ANTS
TERMITES

If ants disappeared from the world, life would change drastically. Many plants depend on seed-eating ants to disperse their seeds. (Some seeds even have ant-sized handles.) Meat-eating ants feed on other insects and spiders. Scavenging ants clean up and recycle dead insects. Ranching ants tend "livestock"—aphids, small insects that live on plant stems—by protecting them from predators. The ants eat the sweet nectar deposited on the plants by the aphids.

Termites are champion recyclers, which is especially important in dry ecosystems, where nothing rots. They eat their way through woody debris, including dead wood and cowpies, returning the nutrients to the soil so that new plants can grow. In some dry ecosystems, termites eat as much as 90 percent of the dead wood and other organic matter. To do this, they rely on tiny creatures that live in their guts, including protozoa, bacteria, and fungi, to help digest the wood. (Imagine living on a diet of toothpicks: termites can!)

Both ants and termites improve the soil by turning it over as they excavate their large underground homes. They build many-chambered nests up to 6 feet deep in the soil, which are connected by tunnels many feet long. (Ants move more soil than earthworms.) Ant and termite

colonies fertilize the soil with underground compost piles of wastes and uneaten food.

Both ants and termites live in colonies with distinct social groups: sterile and flightless females called "workers" and "soldiers," and "queens," who lay eggs. An ant colony begins when a queen lays special eggs that hatch into winged, fertile females and males. These ants fly from the colony, mate, and then drop their wings. The males die after they mate. The females—new queens—dig a nest, lay eggs, and raise their first brood of daughters. The daughters grow into workers and soldiers. Workers gather food, tend their younger sisters, and enlarge the underground nest. Soldiers defend the colony. The queen keeps producing more daughters. When the colony is big enough, she lays a special brood of eggs that hatch into fertile, winged males and females, and the cycle continues.

DANGER!
If you see big—up to an inch long—furry, bright orange-red or white "ants" running on the ground, don't pick them up. Although they are called velvet ants, these insects are actually female wasps with a painful sting.

Many animals, from flickers—large, colorful woodpeckers—to armadillos and bears, dig into ant and termite nests to dine on the plump young. Horned lizards are one of the few animals that eat the tough ant workers.

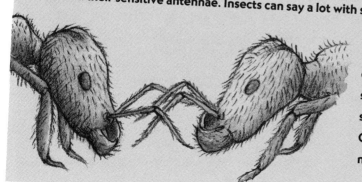

SPEAKING WITH SCENTS. Insects "talk" by spreading chemicals that other insects can smell with their sensitive antennae. Insects can say a lot with scents. Ants can not only tell their sisters where they found food, but how much and what kind it is. If an ant is in danger, she sprays an alarm smell to summon her sisters. Termite soldiers spray enemies with poisons and glues. One kind of termite even has a spray nozzle built into its head!

Bighorn sheep

What Guts!

ONE QUIET FALL AFTERNOON in a desert mountain range, a loud *crack!* splits the silence. Two bighorn sheep, stocky gray-brown animals with huge curving horns on each side of their face, snort and pace away from each other. When the two are

BIGHORN SHEEP
MULE DEER
WHITE-TAILED DEER

about 30 yards apart, each rears up on its hind legs, lowers its head, and rushes forward at speeds of up to 20 miles an hour. Their foreheads collide with a *crack!* loud enough to be heard a mile away. Each sheep staggers from the force of

the blow, then paces off and charges again: *crack!* And again, and again, until one, exhausted, staggers away. The victor snorts loudly, paws the ground, and then ambles off to graze. He has proved his dominance. When the females are ready to mate, he will have his pick.

Bighorn sheep, *borrego* in Spanish (say bore-AY-go), are named for the older males' huge curling horns. They once lived in rocky, inaccessible places throughout the Southwest, from desert cliffs and deep canyons to the steep faces of the highest mountains. But hunting, diseases brought by domestic sheep and goats, and competition with the nonnative animals for food and living space nearly killed them off. Today, bighorn sheep are slowly being reintroduced to the places they once lived.

Deer, on the other hand, are among the Southwest's most commonly seen wild animals. Two kinds of deer live in the region, mule deer and white-tailed deer. Mule deer are more common in the lower elevations, white-tailed deer in the forests of the higher elevations. You can identify mule deer by their donkey-sized ears and their

habit of bouncing away stiff-legged. White-tails hold their white flag of a tail high and trot or gallop away.

Deer browse on woody shrubs as they walk, nipping off a tender branch tip here and there, and use their sensitive lips to pull tender leaves from thorny branches and cactus fruits from the spiny shrubs. Unlike bighorn sheep, deer cannot go without water for long. Deer must drink every day. If they cannot find a water hole, stream, or river, a deer may dig for water in the damp sand of an arroyo, a dry stream channel.

CHEW YOUR FOOD! Deer and bighorn sheep are both ruminants, cud-chewing grazing animals with four-chambered stomachs. Their many stomachs and the microorganisms—microscopic animals—that live in them help ruminants digest truly chewy and downright woody plants. Ruminants also "chew their cud," which means they bring their food up after it has been through their stomachs once, and chew it again. In fact, ruminants chew their food so thoroughly that they eventually wear away their teeth. Pronghorn, elk, and domestic cows and sheep are also ruminants.

HOT TIP!

Bighorn sheep are rare and wary. In the desert, look for them near water holes or *tinajas* (say tee-NA-hahs) in rocky desert mountain ranges, such as at Cabeza Prieta National Wildlife Refuge in extreme southwestern Arizona. Deer are common throughout the Southwest, from the deserts to high in the mountains. Look for them at dawn or dusk, especially near streams.

HOW MUCH WATER IS ENOUGH? Bighorn sheep—and some other desert animals—are so well adapted to desert life that they can go without water for long periods. In fact, bighorns don't need to drink at all. They get enough water from the plants that they graze. And they can survive extreme dehydration—water loss—of over one-fifth of their weight in water. (People die after losing just one-tenth.)

Mule deer

Hippety Hoppers

YOU'LL FIND RABBITS WHEREVER YOU GO in the Southwest, from the hottest deserts to the coldest mountaintops. Long-eared, long-legged jackrabbits lope through dry grasslands and piñon-juniper woodlands. Desert cottontails with fluffy white tails live in desert shrublands. Winter-white snowshoe hares hop on big, furry feet across high-mountain snowdrifts.

Jackrabbit

Jackrabbits are the fastest of Southwest rabbits, loping as fast as 40 miles an hour. They rely on their speed and alertness to escape predators. When pursued, jackrabbits don't just run, they dodge, using their powerful hind legs to

JACKRABBITS
DESERT COTTONTAILS
SNOWSHOE HARES

make sudden zigzagging turns, bound straight up in the air, make midair U-turns, and leap as far as 15 feet in one bound. One jackrabbit predator, the Harris's hawk, outsmarts the speedy jacks by chasing them in teams. One hawk chases the rabbit, then another takes over, and another, until the rabbit tires. Always alert to danger, jackrabbits pick up sound by swiveling their antennaelike ears—equal to one-fifth of their body length—to listen for sounds; their large eyes are positioned high and toward the front of their head to help them see almost all around them without moving.

Desert cottontails are not as speedy as their bigger, long-legged cousins. As a result, many desert predators—from rattlesnakes to coyotes, bobcats, and owls—dine on cottontails. (People do too. Rabbit bones are the most common animal bones found in ruins of ancient southwestern villages; rabbit stew is still a common Southwest dish.) Without predators to control their numbers, desert cottontails breed so quickly that they would overrun their habitat, eat all of the plants, and starve to death.

Desert cottontail

Snowshoe hares live only in the highest mountains in the northern Southwest. Unlike most mountain animals, snowshoe hares don't spend the cold winter months sleeping in a snug den. Instead, they grow an extra-warm coat of snow white winter fur. Their oversized hind feet work like snowshoes, allowing the hare to hop about on the top of the snow, nibbling on plants that stick up through the drifts. Look for snowshoe hares in the Rocky Mountains in southern Colorado and northern New Mexico.

ONE TIMES ONE EQUALS...50,000! Cottontails and jackrabbits are prolific breeders. A cottontail female can bear as many as 30 babies a year. Her children can breed when they are just 10 weeks old, and mate again immediately after giving birth. If all of one cottontail's young survived and produced litters, at the end of her two-year lifetime, she could have 50,000 descendants! Cottontail young are born helpless and furless, with their eyes closed. Jackrabbit young are born ready to run, fully furred, and with their eyes open.

HANDLING THE HEAT Jackrabbits' long ears have another use: they keep these big hares cool. On hot days, jackrabbits sit in the shade and cool themselves as hot blood circulates through the veins in their ears, where it loses heat to outside air. Cottontails stay cool by spending the hot days in an underground burrow, coming out at dusk to browse all night. Many other desert animals pant to cool themselves. When they breathe hot, dry air into their lungs, the moisture in the lungs evaporates. Evaporating the moisture uses energy—heat—from the animal's body, lowering their body temperature. Evaporative coolers chill houses in much the same way.

ROUND-EARED RABBIT What looks like a guinea pig and lives in rockslides near mountaintops in the northern Southwest? A pika, a small rabbit relative with superinsulating fur covering its whole body—even the soles of its feet. They harvest grasses and wildflowers from mountain meadows for winter food. Pikas are also called "coneys," from *conejo* (say cone-AY-hoe), Spanish for "rabbit." Look for drying piles of pika "hay" on rockslides above treeline and listen for their shrill *pee-kah* call.

Hunters!

THE SOUTHWEST IS HOME TO MANY DIFFERENT kinds of hunters, from humans to centipedes. Hunters help keep animal populations in balance, and kill the weak, sick, or old animals, which improves the health of the whole group.

MOUNTAIN LIONS
RATTLESNAKES

The Southwest's largest hunter is the tawny-colored mountain lion. Mountain lions grow as long as 8 feet from nose to tail, and weigh up to 200 pounds. Also called *leones* in Spanish (say lay-OH-nays), they live in many different habitats from Canada to South America. In the Southwest, mountain lions live everywhere, from the desert to the mountaintops, but are most common in the piñon-juniper woodlands of the foothills and mesas.

These big cats hunt deer and may stalk their prey as far as 25 miles. Sometimes they pounce on their victim just like a house cat killing a mouse. Or they perch in a tree hanging over a deer trail and wait for dinner to walk beneath, then drop on the deer and break its neck with their weight. They are not picky: mountain lions hunt animals from the tiniest mice to large elk and cows. They even eat pet cats and dogs.

Mountain lion stalking a white-tailed deer

Rattlesnakes hunt by crawling slowly along the ground and tracking their prey: small animals like lizards, mice, and cottontails. Since rattlers often hunt in the dark, they track the victim's body heat, smell, and vibrations. Rattlesnakes belong to the pit viper group of snakes, which are named for the heat-sensitive pits located on either side of their head between the eye and nostrils. With these heat sensors, rattlesnakes can detect the body heat of a mouse from a foot away.

When a rattler catches its meal, it strikes, injecting venom that paralyzes the animal. As soon as its prey quits struggling, the rattler opens its mouth as wide as it can and swallows the prey whole. By stretching its jaw muscles, a rattler can open its mouth over four times as wide as a person can. Full, the snake rests while its meal digests—sometimes many hours.

Eleven species of rattlesnakes live in the Southwest, more kinds than in any other region of the Americas. The smallest is the tiny, foot-long twin-spotted rattlesnake. The largest is the western diamondback, which can grow to 7 feet long.

BACK OFF! Before a rattlesnake strikes, it vibrates the horny buttons at the end of its tail to say, "Back off!" A Pima Indian story from Arizona explains why: Rattlesnake used to be the gentlest animal because Sun God forgot to give him a weapon to protect himself. The animals liked to hear him rattle, so they teased him all the time. Sun God felt sorry for the snake and told him, "Get two sharp thorns from the devil's claw plant and put them in your mouth." Rattlesnake did as he was told. "Now," said Sun God, "you will have to rattle to give a warning. Strike only if you have to." The next time the animals teased him, Rattlesnake rattled his warning. They didn't stop, so he struck. After that every animal heeded his rattle. To this day, say the Pimas, Rattlesnake strikes only if he has to, but everyone fears him.

DANGER!

Rattlesnakes and mountain lions can be dangerous. But they rarely kill people. Rattlesnakes bite about 1,000 people a year in the United States, and fewer than 10 of those die. If you see or hear a rattler, stop. Look for it and back away. A rattlesnake is just as eager to avoid you as you are to avoid it.

Out of hundreds of encounters between humans and mountain lions in the past 20 years, only a handful of people have been attacked. In 1990, a mountain lion killed a jogger above Colorado Springs, Colorado. (That same year, domestic dogs killed six people in the Southwest.) The best way to avoid a lion attack is to not hike alone. These big cats only attack solitary prey.

Love Bites

YOU ARE A TINY MALE BLACK WIDOW SPIDER, and you are approaching your intended mate. She, three times your size, with a venomous bite, sits in the center of her web, alert for prey. How do you court her without being eaten? Cautiously.

Black widow spiders are named for the female's habit of eating anything that hits her web, including her mate. After the male sneaks

BLACK WIDOW SPIDERS
TARANTULA SPIDERS

up on his intended and mates with her, he may become dinner himself. That's okay, because the nutrition that the female gets from eating the male helps ensure that her eggs will be healthy. In effect, the male gives his life to ensure his children's survival.

Female black widows are master insect-catchers. When the vibrations of her net tell her that an insect has hit, the spider flings her silken strands around the victim, entrapping it. (A strand of black widow spider silk is stronger than a strand of steel of the same thickness.) Then she approaches and bites her prey, injecting poisons that paralyze and liquefy the soft parts of her victim so that the toothless spider can sip it like a milkshake. She may eat 2,000 insects, from house flies to beetles, during her year-long life.

With a legspan of up to 6 inches, big hairy brown bodies, and oversized fangs, tarantula spiders look ferocious. Appearances are deceiving. Tarantulas are actually harmless to humans. Their venom is mild and their nature gentle. They are North America's largest spiders, common throughout the desert and dry lowlands of the Southwest.

Unlike black widows, tarantulas don't build webs to capture prey. Instead, they hunt actively at night, sniffing and tapping around for a meal. They mostly hunt insects, small lizards, and sometimes other tarantulas. These big spiders rush their prey, killing it with a

DANGER!
Female black widows make one of the world's most potent venoms. Desert Native Americans once used crushed black widow bodies to poison their arrows. But you are more likely to be killed by lightning in the Southwest than by a black widow spider's bite. Only the females, coal black with a red, violin-shaped marking on their abdomen, are dangerous—males have no venom. Females won't bite except to defend themselves or their eggs. Look for their irregular webs in dark, sheltered places in garages, under porches, or at the entrances to rodent burrows throughout the Southwest, except at high elevations.

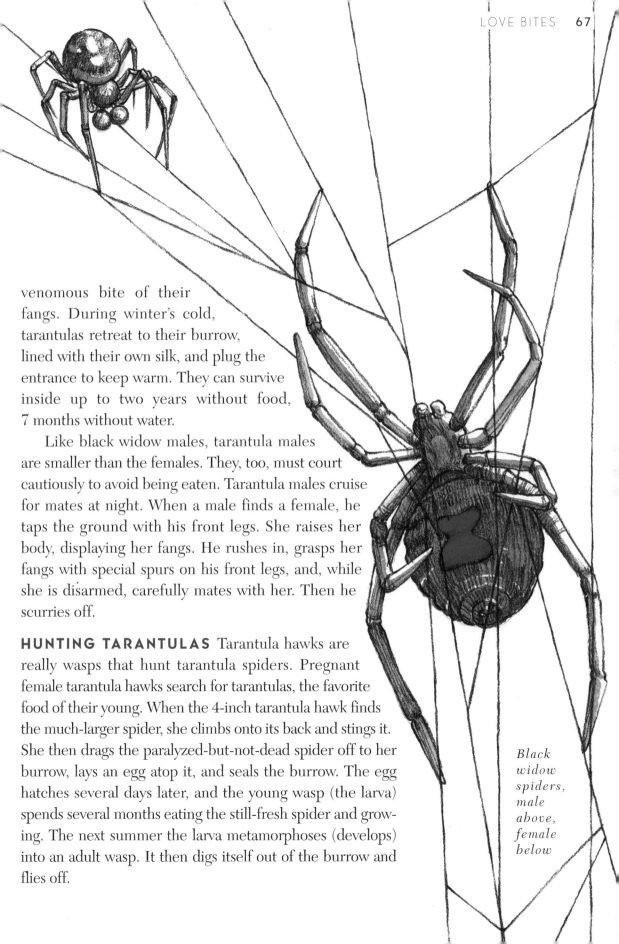

venomous bite of their
fangs. During winter's cold,
tarantulas retreat to their burrow,
lined with their own silk, and plug the
entrance to keep warm. They can survive
inside up to two years without food,
7 months without water.

Like black widow males, tarantula males
are smaller than the females. They, too, must court
cautiously to avoid being eaten. Tarantula males cruise
for mates at night. When a male finds a female, he
taps the ground with his front legs. She raises her
body, displaying her fangs. He rushes in, grasps her
fangs with special spurs on his front legs, and, while
she is disarmed, carefully mates with her. Then he
scurries off.

HUNTING TARANTULAS Tarantula hawks are
really wasps that hunt tarantula spiders. Pregnant
female tarantula hawks search for tarantulas, the favorite
food of their young. When the 4-inch tarantula hawk finds
the much-larger spider, she climbs onto its back and stings it.
She then drags the paralyzed-but-not-dead spider off to her
burrow, lays an egg atop it, and seals the burrow. The egg
hatches several days later, and the young wasp (the larva)
spends several months eating the still-fresh spider and growing. The next summer the larva metamorphoses (develops)
into an adult wasp. It then digs itself out of the burrow and
flies off.

*Black
widow
spiders,
male
above,
female
below*

Night Hunters

THE SUN SETS AT THE END OF A SUMMER DAY in the desert. Darkness falls and the air grows cooler. Soon the night is alive with noises: squeals and rustles, the *crunch, crunch* of hooves, deep-voiced hoots, high-pitched chattering. . . . Who hunts at night?

BATS
OWLS
SCORPIONS

Between April and October, when night-flying insects are active, bats are one of the most commonly spotted night hunters. Looking like mice with leathery wings, bats are the only mammals that can fly. (Mammals are animals like humans that have backbones, nurse their young, and are able to heat or cool their bodies themselves.) North America's smallest bats, western pipistrelles, are among the Southwest's bat species. These tiny bats have walnut-sized bodies and weigh about as much as a penny.

People are sometimes scared of bats, but North American bats are not harmful to humans. In fact, bats consume tons of flying insects that "bug" people, including mosquitos and moths. Mouse-eared bats, the most widely distributed species of bat in North America, can consume 600 mosquitoes an hour! Not all southwestern bats eat insects. Pallid bats hunt the desert and dry grasslands at night for larger prey, including scorpions. Long-nosed bats hover to slurp sweet nectar from the flowers of giant cactus and century plants. Sadly, pesticides—chemicals that kill insects—and disturbance by people are killing off the Southwest's bats.

Owl

Owls, like bats, are real night creatures. Owls spend daytime hours snoozing in a tree or tall cactus, camouflaged by the streaks and dots of their bark-colored plumage. At dusk, they wake up and begin looking around for prey. (Owls can turn their head completely around to see behind them.) They then fly off to hunt. If an owl flies past you in the dark, you won't hear it because its feathers are designed to not

Thousands of free-tailed bats roost in the miles of underground passageways of Carlsbad Caverns, in southern New Mexico. On summer evenings, you can watch the hordes of bats exit the caves in a whirling cloud. Five to ten thousand bats fly out each minute, spiraling in a counter-clockwise column that is visible from miles away.

DANGER! Scorpions sting humans only in self-defense. Most species' stings are like a bad bee sting. But the stings of one of the smallest scorpions, the 2 3/4-inch-long bark scorpion of the Sonoran Desert of Arizona and northern Mexico, can kill a person. Bark scorpions hide under logs or underground.

make noise. This allows them to surprise their prey.

Among the Southwest's 13 species of owls is the world's smallest owl, the fist-sized elf owl, which stands just under 6 inches tall. Elf owls live in holes drilled by woodpeckers in the trunks of giant cacti, sycamores, and cottonwood trees. One Southwest owl, the burrowing owl, is unusual: it lives in the ground and is often active in daytime. These long-legged owls occupy abandoned prairie dog or ground squirrel burrows, and drainpipes on buildings.

Scorpions are strictly nocturnal, emerging to hunt in large numbers on warm nights. These relatives of spiders look like miniature lobsters with two long-clawed pincers and a segmented "tail" curving back over their body and ending in a needlelike stinger. Most scorpions are less than 3 inches long, but one Southwest scorpion, the giant desert hairy scorpion, grows to 5 1/2 inches long. Scorpions hunt other ground-dwelling critters like insects, centipedes, and millipedes. They catch their prey in their pincers and quickly paralyze it with a flick of their stinger, injecting a dose of poison.

NIGHT VISION Contrary to the saying "blind as a bat," bats have excellent vision. They "see" in the dark using echolocation—they bounce high-pitched sounds off nearby objects to pinpoint their location. Owls' eyes are large and designed for night vision. Their facial feathers, arranged like twin disks around their eyes, act like sound-collecting dish antennae, picking up sounds and directing them to owls' ears. Although scorpions possess at least three pairs of eyes, they feel their way in the dark using sensitive organs on their legs and sensitive body hairs.

Rock Sculptures

ARCHES, NATURAL BRIDGES
BALANCED ROCKS
FINS, HOODOOS

Double-O Arch,
Arches National Park, Utah

DOUBLE-O ARCH, RAINBOW BRIDGE, Fairy Castle, Cochise's Head. . . . The Southwest boasts more "rock sculptures"—rocks carved into fantastic shapes by erosion—than anywhere else in North America, if not the world. Most of the Southwest's natural sculpture gardens are found on the Colorado Plateau.

Rock sculptures come in many shapes: arches, natural bridges (arches carved by streams), balanced rocks, fins (thin walls of rock that stand up like the fins on a fish's back), and hoodoos ("crowds" of eroded spires and pillars). Water begins the sculpturing process when it trickles into cracks in the rocks. As it freezes in the cracks each winter, water expands and pries off loose pieces of rock, widening the cracks. Growing plant roots pry the cracks apart, too. Eventually, the cracks grow wide enough that wind, carrying sand, blows in and rasps away at the rock. Together, water, plant roots, and wind sculpt the rock, eventually creating free-standing spires, fins, buttes, or crowds of hoodoos out of solid rock. Where holes pierce rock walls, arches and natural bridges form.

HOT TIP!

You can camp among a "forest" of toadstool-shaped hoodoos at City of Rocks State Park in southwestern New Mexico. Goblin Valley State Reserve, southwest of Green River, Utah, boasts crowds of goblin-shaped rocks.

The largest number of natural arches in North America—around 1,800 sandstone arches—are within Arches National Park, just north of Moab, Utah, on the Colorado Plateau. Arches is home to Landscape Arch, one of the world's largest, more than eight stories high and spanning 290 feet, and Double-O Arch, a rare double arch. Nearby Canyonlands National Park also contains many fantastic spires, fins, and buttes. A crowd of spires striped soft pink and white, like giant candy sticks, dominate the Needles area of Canyonlands. Bryce Canyon and Zion national parks, Monument Valley Tribal Park, and Natural Bridges National Monument—all on the Colorado Plateau—also protect spectacular rock sculptures.

One other area of the Southwest, Chiricahua National Monument in southeastern Arizona, is known for its spectacular hoodoos. (*Chiricahua* means "land of the standing-up rocks" in Apache.) Thousands of towering rock spires, weird figures, and giant balanced rocks crowd the mountain slopes. Look for Big Balanced Rock, weighing 1,000 tons—as much as 500 elephants!—which rests on a base just 4 feet thick.

Big Balanced Rock

HOW THE ANIMALS TURNED TO STONE A Paiute Indian story tells how crowds of bizarrely shaped rocks at Bryce Canyon National Park in Utah formed. The lizards, birds, and other animals that once lived at Bryce had the power to make themselves look like people. But they behaved badly, angering Shin-Owav, a Paiute god. So Shin-Owav turned them into rocks. If you look closely, you can see the animals-as-people—dancing, gambling, and gossiping—in the rock spires.

YOU CAN DO IT! To see how erosion affects different kinds of rocks, you need shallow bowls, sand, sugar cubes, clay, and a watering can. First, make your "rock" sculptures. Put a couple of handfuls of sand in one bowl, wet it, and mold the sand into a fin or a flat-topped mesa. In another bowl, stack the sugar cubes to form your own balanced rock. In another bowl, mold an arch from the clay. Then fill the watering can with water, and sprinkle "rain" on your sculptures. Start with the sand. What happens? Sand erodes easily, like shales and mudstones (both are rocks that literally wash away with each rain). Then water the sugar cubes. Is more rain needed before they begin to dissolve? The sugar cubes act like limestone, a kind of rock that seems hard but can be slowly dissolved by water. Next, "rain" on the clay. What happens? Dried clay acts like sandstone and other hard rocks—it erodes so slowly that you can't see it happen.

Sky Islands

WHEN YOU IMAGINE THE SOUTHWEST, what do you see? A hot, dry place? A bare landscape, home mostly to lizards and cacti? Much of the Southwest fits that description. But not all. The region also includes high mountain ranges and plateaus (tablelands) that rise abruptly from the dry lowlands. Because their heights snag more rain and snow than the dry country below, their slopes and canyons provide green and cool refuges for a host of animals and plants that cannot survive in the deserts. Isolated by the hot, dry country around them, these high refuges are called "sky islands."

Porcupine

BEARS
PORCUPINES
MONKEYFLOWERS
PAINTBRUSH

In the Southwest, black bears, the smallest and most common bears in North America, live only on the sky islands. They spend the warm parts of the year foraging for foods like wild honeybee hives, berries, roots, and ground squirrels. They must store up enough body fat to keep them alive through their long winter's sleep in an underground den. In dry years, when wild food is in short supply, black bears often move into towns, poaching from gardens and trash bins. Although black bears adapt well to town life, people don't adapt well to them—urban bears are often killed. Black bears, *el oso negro* in Spanish (say ELL OH-so NAY-grow), stand 2 to 3 feet high at the shoulder and weigh up to 400 pounds. Despite their name, they grow cinnamon brown as well as black fur.

Porcupines are another distinctive sky island resident. These rodents—buck-toothed relatives of mice and beavers—are armed with long, barbed quills over their head, back, and upper tail. They look fearsome, but are actually slow and shy. Strict vegetarians, porcupines waddle about, munching on leaves, berries, and

HOT TIP!

Look for "gardens" of wildflowers in meadows and along streams of sky islands, especially on the Grand Canyon's North Rim in Arizona, in the Sangre de Cristo Mountains in northern New Mexico (named "Christ's blood" for the red glow the mountains cast at sunset), and in the Henry Mountains and La Sal Mountains of southern Utah.

seeds, and chewing the sweet inner bark of trees. Contrary to many tales, porcupines cannot throw their quills. But the quills do detach easily when the porcupine thrashes around. The white, hollow lower part of the quill is used in traditional Native American art, decorating deerskin moccasins, clothing, and pouches.

Wildflowers abound in the cooler, moister conditions of sky islands. One easily identified wildflower, the monkeyflower, a relative of snapdragons, is named for the red spots that look like a monkey face on the lower lip of its two-lipped flower. Monkeyflower plants are usually yellow (rarely pink), grow from 2 inches to 3 feet tall, and are found near water, from the tiniest seeps to small streams. Another wildflower, paintbrush, is named for the colorful leaves that make the upper part of the plant look as if had been dipped into vivid pink, red, orange, or yellow paint. Paintbrush is a parasite, a plant whose roots tap other plants' roots for food and water. It taps into sagebrush, agave, and grass roots.

WATERMELON SNOW High-country snowbanks that turn pink in summer are called "watermelon snow" for their watermelony smell, taste, and color. The color and flavor come from a minute alga—a microscopic plant—that grows in the meltwater on the surface of the snow.

MAROONED Like islands in the ocean, sky islands are often home to endemic species, plants or animals that live nowhere else. For instance, a salamander called the Jemez Mountains salamander was more widely distributed when climates were cooler during the ice ages. As climates grew warmer and drier, the salamander was marooned on the Jemez Mountains—its "island." Eventually it evolved into a distinct species, adapted only to its tiny mountain range.

Indian Paintbrush

Trash Collectors

PACKRATS
MAGPIES

JUST AS SOME PEOPLE ARE COLLECTORS, stashing away enormous quantities of "junk," so, too, are some animals. Packrats, animals that look like large mice with rounded ears, twitching whiskers, and a long, furry tail, are named for their habit of collecting anything small enough to carry away, including shiny objects like jewelry and coins. Packrats, also called trade rats or woodrats, also collect sticks, grass, spiny cactus pads, cowpies, feathers, bones, and aluminum cans. They use these treasures to build large nests in buildings, in crevices in rocks, at the base of trees and large shrubs, and in caves.

Packrats' huge mounded nests—up to 5 feet high and 2 1/2 feet across—act as insulation, keeping them cool in summer and warm in winter. (Inside one desert nest, the temperature never rose above 88 degrees F, even though the ground outside reached 167 degrees!) The trash also acts as armor. Cactus pads, pieces of glass, and jagged strips of aluminum cans may cover the nest, perhaps protecting it from being torn apart by predators such as owls and coyotes.

Magpies—striking black-and-white birds with streaming, foot-long tails and harsh voices—also collect shiny objects. Magpies have been known to pick up and carry away watches, eyeglasses, can lids, and coins. Like other

YOU CAN DO IT!
There is enough trash around the Southwest to supply all the packrats and magpies in the world and then some. You can help clean up the Southwest by picking up trash wherever you see it. How many bags can you fill in one outing?

Magpie

Packrat

corvids—relatives of crows and ravens—magpies are smart. They mimic many sounds in their calls and can even learn human words. Magpies also adapt well to human habitat, often living around farms and towns.

Like packrats, magpies build huge nests, 2 to 4 feet high. Unlike packrats' loose junk heaps, however, magpie nests are in trees and are carefully built of sticks and grasses cemented with mud. Nest building is part of magpies' courtship ritual. The male magpie brings gifts of nesting material to the female; she builds the nest herself. Unlike packrats, magpies abandon their nests when they become too trashy. Other birds, from owls and hawks to bluebirds, move into abandoned magpie nests.

Black-billed magpies, the magpies of the Southwest, eat almost everything, although they usually feed on insects picked up on the ground. Black-billed magpies once followed the huge herds of bison that roamed the Great Plains, plucking ticks and other insects from the huge beasts' fur and devouring grasshoppers stirred up by the herds.

READING TRASH Packrat nests are used by generation after generation of these rodents. Packrats periodically clean house, carrying the "trash" to a nearby place, trampling it flat, and urinating on it. Over time, they build a layered packrat landfill, a record of what packrats have eaten and picked up around their nests for thousands of years. Biologists have learned to read the layers of packrat landfills in order to tell what plants grew nearby, just as archaeologists—scientists who study ancient peoples—excavate trash dumps to read ancient peoples' lives. Piñon pinecones and juniper berries in ancient packrat middens show that these trees once grew where deserts now spread. Reading packrat trash thus tells us that Southwest climates were much cooler long ago.

HOT TIP!

Look for packrat nests throughout the lower elevations of the Southwest, from the hot deserts to the piñon-juniper woodlands of the foothills and lower mesas. Packrats often build nests in the bases of spiny plants like mesquite shrubs and prickly pear cacti. Magpies are birds of the northern Southwest. Look for their big, untidy nests in cottonwood trees in valley bottoms and around farms.

Horned lizard

Leaping Lizards

ONE IS LARGE, QUICK, AND BRIGHTLY COLORED, and hunts on the run. The other is small, slow, and earth-colored, and hunts by holding still.

They're both lizards. The common collared lizard, named for two black "collars" ringing its neck, is the eye-catching speedster. Its neon-bright coloring—a brilliant emerald belly with touches of turquoise blue, and chrome yellow accents above—screams to be noticed. Collared lizards grow to a foot long—at least half of which is tail.

Collared lizards live on rocky areas throughout the lower and mid-elevations of the Southwest, but are most often seen in the slickrock country of the Colorado Plateau. These large lizards need plenty of bare rock—open areas for running and boulders for basking in the sun and using as lookout posts. Collared lizards hunt on the run, often racing on their hind legs with their long tail raised, leaping nimbly from rock to rock as they chase insects and smaller lizards. Lizards and other reptiles don't heat or cool themselves from within like people do. To warm themselves, lizards rely on the sun, spending lots of time soaking up the rays. To cool off, they take to the shade.

Horned lizards are as different as can be from their

COLOR CODES

Collared lizards "talk" with their colors. Like other brightly colored lizards, they intimidate challengers by "pumping"— doing push-ups to flash the neon-bright colors of their chest and throat. Collared lizards' colors come from the foods that they eat. If they are eating well, their colors are bright; if not, they lose their brilliance. Thus, the brightness of their colors tells potential mates how good they are at surviving. Other lizards, and some fish and birds, also speak with colors.

COLLARED LIZARDS
HORNED LIZARDS

flashy and quick cousins. They are short, growing to no more than 6 inches long, and squat, with a body shaped like a hockey puck and crowned with a collar of spines behind their head. They are also called horny toads because their flattened body looks toadlike.

The horned lizard's main strategy for survival is camouflage, an ability to blend in with its surroundings. Most lizards rely on speed to avoid predators and to catch their meals, but not horned lizards. They hide by holding still instead. A horned lizard's body color matches the color of the soil where it lives—pale buff to yellow-brown to reddish to nearly black. Unevenly shaped dark spots on their back mimic shadows; fringelike scales edging their body break up their outline. A motionless horned lizard looks just like a small rock.

If a predator does discover a fat horned lizard, it doesn't necessarily become dinner. These little lizards can inflate themselves by gulping air like a blowfish, making their spiny bodies very difficult to swallow. One species even startles attackers by squirting them with a stream of blood from a pore in its eyelid!

MONSTERS! The Southwest's biggest lizard is a monster of sorts. Up to 2 feet long, with a heavy body, sausagelike tail, and beaded skin striped orange and black, the Gila (say HEE-la) monster is truly odd-looking. It is also one of only two venomous—poison-bearing—lizards in the world. Unique to the Sonoran and Chihuahuan deserts, Gila monsters are slow-moving and surprisingly gentle. But when provoked, they hiss fiercely, lunge, and bite, dripping venom into the wound. Although painful, Gila bites are usually not fatal to humans. These lumbering lizards eat the eggs and young of ground-dwelling birds and desert tortoises. When food is short, they live on fat stored in their tail.

ANT KILLERS

Horned lizards eat ants. Sadly, horned lizard populations are endangered in parts of Texas. There, pesticides—poisonous chemicals—sprayed to kill ants cause horny toads to starve. People also capture horned lizards for pets. But the little lizards usually starve in captivity, because it is hard to catch the hundreds of ants they need to eat each day.

Gila monster

Stinkers

SMELLING FUNNY AND TASTING BITTER help the creosote bush, one of the commonest plants in the lower elevations of the southern Southwest, survive in the hot, dry desert environment. In fact, these tough plants outlive all other desert dwellers. A creosote bush called "King Clone" growing in the Mojave desert of southern California has been dated at 10,000 years old, making it the oldest living plant known.

CREOSOTE BUSH SAGEBRUSH

Creosote bush is a wiry shrub with small, shiny evergreen leaves, scraggly black stems, yellow flowers, and fuzzy, white fruits that look like cottonballs. It forms seas of olive green that cover miles and miles of the Chihuahuan, Sonoran, and Mojave deserts.

Creosote bush is also called *hediondilla* (say ay-dee-ohn-DEE-ya), "little stinker," because after a summer rain it fills the air with a peculiar smell—a sweet, resiny, tarry, medicinal perfume. The scent comes from over 40 volatile oils, stinky chemicals that wash off into the air when rain wets the plant. Creosote's odor may help protect it from hungry animals. In case the smell doesn't do the trick, creosote bush also employs an armor of waxy sap that tastes terrible. If a grazer does chow down on creosote bush, the wax forms an indigestible lump in the animal's gut, causing a stomach ache worse than what happens when you eat too many doughnuts.

Big sagebrush is the "stinker" of the northern Southwest, replacing creosote bush in the shrublands of the Great Basin Desert and the valleys of the Rocky Mountains. It, too, fills the air with its trademark perfume after rains. Called *chamisa hediondo* (say cha-MEE-sah ay-dee-OHN-do), "stinking bush" in Spanish, big sagebrush grows from 2 to 7 feet tall, with many branches coming from a single twisting trunk. Its small, felt-covered leaves give the plant its characteristic gray-green color. The hairy coating is the plant's protection against sunburn. (All desert plants must protect themselves from sunburn.)

Like creosote bush, sagebrush employs fragrant chemical weapons to ward off grazers. But

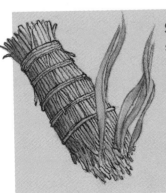

SACRED SMOKE The pungent smoke of burning sagebrush is used as a cleanser in many Native American ceremonies. Native Americans young and old cleanse their bodies and minds by sitting in sweat lodges, small ceremonial structures heated by red-hot rocks. Sweating and breathing in the sagebrush-scented smoke is a purifying ritual.

Sagebrush

some animals, including deer and jackrabbits, aren't discouraged. One kind of bird, the plump, long-tailed sage grouse, dines almost exclusively on sagebrush. Big sagebrush is the largest of half a dozen species of sagebrush found in the Southwest. Sagebrush covers over half of the area of the western United States.

FIRE! Chiles, hot fruits used to flavor Mexican cooking, contain capsaicins, one of the most potent chemical weapons of all plants. These odorless, colorless, tasteless chemicals make you feel pain. When you bite into a chile, the capsaicins set off fire alarms in your mouth, and make you sweat. Wild chiles, called *piquins* (say pee-KEENS) in the Southwest, are the hottest of the chile peppers, containing 39,000 times the amount of capsaicins needed to tell your taste buds that you've bitten into a chile! Chiles probably developed capsaicins to keep mammals from eating the fleshy fruit.

HOT TIP!

Buffalo gourd, a sprawling vine that grows in the Southwest's deserts and dry grasslands, grows softball-sized green- or yellow-striped gourds that look like small melons. But don't try to eat these "melons"—they contain the bitterest substances known to humans. Eating the fruit causes nausea, severe stomach cramps, and diarrhea. In northern Mexico, the gourds are called *chichicoyotas* (say chee-chee-coy-OH-tahs), "trickster breasts," because, the story goes, mothers wean their babies by rubbing the bitter fruits on their breasts.

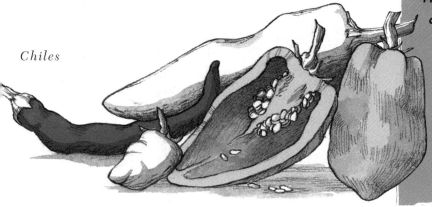

Chiles

Cow with devil's claw pod

Hitchhiking Seeds

PLANTS ARE ROOTED IN PLACE, unable to move except to sway with the wind. How do they make sure that their seeds reach places where they can sprout and grow?

Plants cope with the problem of spreading their seeds in fascinating ways. Some plants, like devil's claw, a sprawling plant of the southern Southwest, hitch rides on passing animals (including humans!). These kinds of plants grow pods covered with hooks, spines, or prickles around their seeds. When a passing animal brushes against the spiny pods, the pods hook onto the animal's fur (or people's clothing) or attach themselves to the animal's skin, and ride along to distant places.

DEVIL'S CLAW
GOATSBEARD
WILD RASPBERRY

Devil's claw is named for its seed pod. At first, the plump green pods look like fat, bumpy okra pods, except that they end in a thick, curving claw up to 5 inches long. As the pods dry out, they turn black. The claw splits in two, each half curving like an elephant tusk. These twin prongs

SEEING RED

Many plants that grow edible fruits use color to attract fruit-eaters. Wild chiles, for instance, attract birds with their bright orange-red color. Birds cannot see all the colors that humans do, but can distinguish red.

catch the legs of passersby like an ankle bracelet. The animal carries the pod along, spreading seeds far and wide. Devil's claw grows in the deserts and dry grasslands of the southern Southwest, from west Texas to southern Arizona and northern Mexico.

Other plants, like goatsbeard, grow seeds that can float on the wind. These seeds are light and sprout wings, feathery tails, or parachutelike structures that help the seeds float away on passing breezes. Goatsbeard's seeds form a ball-shaped seed head similar to a dandelion's. Each seed is attached to a slender stalk ending in a cluster of feathery branches, which look like a parachute turned inside out. The cluster of feathery branches carry the seed far from its parent, drifting on the slightest breeze.

Goatsbeard seed head

Although it is common throughout the Southwest, goatsbeard is not a native. Like tumbleweed, dandelions, and other nonnative plants, goatsbeard has spread far and wide. Goatsbeard grows in places where the soil has been disturbed, like towns and roadsides. Its stem grows about 2 feet tall, with long, slender grasslike leaves, and ends in a single yellow flower that looks like a dandelion.

Some plant seeds hitch a ride in the stomachs of animals. These plants, including wild raspberries, bury their seeds in sweet-tasting fruit. Animals devour the fruit. But, because the seeds have a hard coating that protects them from being digested in the animal's gut, they pass through and are deposited in a pat of "fertilizer"—animal scat—that helps them sprout and grow.

Wild raspberries grow in the foothills, high mesas, and mountains of the Southwest, in sunny spots in the forests. Their spiny branches may reach 9 feet tall. Their white, five-petaled flowers grow into sweet, many-seeded ruby red berries the size of gumdrops. One species, the New Mexico raspberry, is found only in the Southwest. It grows in southern New Mexico, southern Arizona, and northern Mexico.

YOU CAN DO IT! Plant seeds and their pods or fruits have long provided food and fibers to Southwest peoples. Black fibers from devil's claw pods, for instance, are used by Tohono O'odham, Pima, and Havasupai basket makers to add black designs to their baskets. To find the fibers yourself, open a dried devil's claw pod by pulling on the two horns. Then strip off the hard outer covering. Inside, the pod is lined with fibers. Carefully peel off a few fibers. Can you twist them into a cord? Is it strong? Flexible?

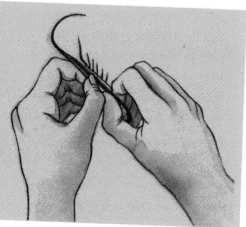

Transformers

HAVE YOU EVER WATCHED TADPOLES—those tiny, dark wriggling creatures that are all head and tail—swimming in a puddle or pond? Some of the tadpoles are bigger, with swollen bodies and four tiny legs. What is happening to their bodies?

They are transforming, growing into frogs. All amphibians are transformers. They hatch from eggs laid in ponds, puddles, streams, or other watery places. When young, amphibians breathe through special structures called gills and can survive only in water. They eat and grow for days, weeks, or months—depending on the species—and then begin a slow transformation: their body swells to accommodate lungs. Their legs grow; their gills vanish. Eventually, they hop or crawl out of the water and breathe air through lungs.

LEOPARD FROGS
TIGER SALAMANDERS

Because amphibian young must live in water, these transformers are at a disadvantage in the dry Southwest. How do they cope? Most, like leopard frogs, small, 2- to 5-inch-long, green or olive brown frogs with bulging eyes and dark spots on their backs, don't stray far from permanent water. Still, leopard frogs are widespread in the Southwest, living from the

Tiger salamander

hottest, low deserts to above treeline in the highest mountains, wherever water is found.

Six kinds of leopard frogs live in the Southwest. Each is adapted to one particular geographic area. For example, the lowland leopard frog lives in the lower elevations of the southern Southwest, where climates are hotter and drier. With warm weather for more of the year, lowland leopard frogs may breed twice, once in early spring, once in fall. Living in the colder conditions of the mountains and plateaus of the northern Southwest, the northern leopard frog only has time for one generation to mature before ponds and streams freeze over.

Caterpillar

Tiger salamanders, another Southwest amphibian, live near water but, like spadefoot toads (see *Sudden Surprises*, page 84), spend much of their adult lives burrowed underground, where they are less likely to dry out. Tiger salamanders don't dig their own burrows, however. They "borrow" vacant burrows dug by other animals. They emerge from underground and enter the water for mating and laying their eggs. Their aquatic young are called "mudpuppies" or "water dogs."

Tiger salamanders grow up to a foot long and are the Southwest's largest amphibian. Named for the tiger-stripe pattern of their smooth, shiny skin, they are stout creatures with a broad head, small eyes, and a long tail.

Cocoon

WHY ARE THE FROGS DYING? Frogs and toads are disappearing across the Southwest, and all over the world. Biologists are worried. What is happening? A virus—a microscopic, disease-causing critter—seems to be the cause. But biologists are not sure why the virus, which has always lived in the frogs and toads, is now killing them. Many think that environmental problems—like air and/or water pollution, the thinning of the ozone layer, or habitat loss—make frogs and toads more vulnerable to a virus that they normally could survive.

Monarch Butterfly

OTHER TRANSFORMERS Some kinds of insects transform themselves, too. Butterflies, for example, spend much of their life as many-legged, earthbound caterpillars. The caterpillar munches on plants and grows . . . and grows . . . and grows . . . until it is ready to spin a cocoon, a case in which it hides while it transforms into a winged butterfly.

Sudden Surprises

MUCH OF THE SOUTHWEST IS DRY, so dry that water is rare and precious. But when the rains do come, new lives suddenly appear while the world is wet, including bleating spadefoot toads, tiny fairy shrimp, and short-lived annual wildflowers.

HOT TIP!

The best spring wildflower shows occur in the Sonoran Desert of Arizona and northern Sonora, Mexico. Since rainfall varies greatly from place to place, wildflower displays vary too.

   Try Organ Pipe Cactus National Monument in southwestern Arizona or Saguaro National Park near Tucson. Or the Desert Botanical Garden in Phoenix, where regular watering guarantees spring wildflowers.

SPADEFOOT TOADS
FAIRY SHRIMP
ANNUAL WILDFLOWERS

Spadefoot toads, small toads from 1 1/2 to 3 1/2 inches long, appear like magic on wet summer nights throughout the lower elevations of the Southwest. They fill the night air with their curious trills and bleats, calling for mates. As soon as puddles dry out, however, the tiny *sapitos* (say sah-PEE-toes)—"little toads" in Spanish—vanish as suddenly as they came.

Where do they come from and where do they go? Spadefoot toads spend most of their lives dug as deep as 3 feet underground, protected from drying out. After thunderstorms, spadefoots dig out briefly. They catch insects with their long, sticky tongues, and they find mates. At dawn, the little toads dig themselves back into the soil, leaving behind egg masses floating in rainwater puddles and ponds. (Like all toads, spadefoot toads are amphibians, animals that change from gilled, water-dwelling creatures to lung-breathing land-dwellers. See *Transformers*, page 82.) Before the puddles dry out, the new generation of toads must race through the aquatic part of their life, speeding from egg to tadpole to toad. One kind of spadefoot toad matures in just 10 days. Bullfrogs, by contrast, take two years to develop!

Rainwater puddles and ponds explode with other tiny lives. Among these instant residents are fairy shrimp—miniature relatives of horseshoe crabs. Fairy shrimp hatch from special, thick-walled eggs that can survive for *decades* in cracks in the soil, waiting for a puddle to form. After hatching, these transparent

YOU CAN DO IT! In summer, dip water from a rainwater puddle or pool with a cup and look at it through a magnifying glass. Watch for movement. Fairy shrimp are clear and swim about on their back, propelling themselves with 22 miniature legs. Tadpoles are black, and seem to be all head, bulging eyes, and wriggling tail. Tiny, rounded springtails hop on the water's surface. Slimy green mats are algae, water-dwelling plants.

creatures about the size of a thumbnail swim about on their backs, feeding on microscopic food stirred up by their 11 pairs of legs. Their whole life cycle lasts about two weeks, the average life of a good-sized desert puddle.

Animals are not the only desert residents to take advantage of the rare times that water is abundant. When winter rains and snows soak the deserts of the southern Southwest, wildflower seeds respond, sprouting as soon as soils warm up the following spring. Like fairy shrimp, these plants fit their whole lives into the few weeks that the soil remains moist. They sprout by the billions, grow, bloom, produce a new generation of seeds, and die when the soil dries out again. Their blossoms paint the desert with a vivid carpet of orange, yellow, pink, and violet-blue, and then vanish as quickly as they appeared. The seeds that they leave behind may "wait" years before conditions are just right for them to germinate and continue the cycle.

HERE TODAY, GONE TOMORROW *Playas* (say PLY-uhs), Spanish for "beaches," are flat-floored lake beds common in the southern and western Southwest. After heavy summer rains or spring snowmelts, playas fill with a few inches of water, forming shallow lakes. The water often lasts just a week or two. But during their short lives, playa lakes are home to a host of creatures, like fairy shrimp.

Spadefoot toad

Swell Swimmers

WATER IS RARE IN THE SOUTHWEST. But where it occurs, the Southwest's rivers and streams are home to amazing creatures, from playful river otters and huge fish to tiny insects called backswimmers.

RIVER OTTERS
COLORADO SQUAWFISH
COMMON BACKSWIMMERS

River otters are the Southwest's water acrobats. They swim right side up, upside down, or sideways. They can undulate like a fish, using their heavy tail as a rudder, make sudden U-turns, dive as deep as 40 feet, and race one another. These playful animals make slides in muddy or icy streambanks by loping up the bank, flopping on their belly, then sliding with a "splash" into the water.

River otters are made for life in the water. Their body—up to 3 feet long, including a foot or more of tail—is covered in thick, water-repellent, chocolate brown fur that keeps them warm even in near-freezing water. Their short, strong legs end in webbed toes. River otters use their swimming skills to hunt fish, frogs, turtles, and other aquatic life. Although they once swam in rivers and streams throughout the Southwest, river otters are now endangered in Arizona and Colorado, and rare in the rest of the region.

> **HOT TIP!**
>
> The best place to see river otters splash and play is at the Arizona-Sonora Desert Museum, just west of Tucson, Arizona. (See *The Wild Inside*, page 98.)

The Southwest's largest swimming creature (besides people) is the Colorado squawfish, which can grow to 6 feet long and weigh up to 80 pounds. These giant gray-green and silver fish are unique to the Colorado River and its tributaries, where they swim in deep pools and catch smaller fish. Like river otters, Colorado squawfish were once widespread and are now endangered. Dams and withdrawal of water for irrigation have shrunk their habitat to only a few parts of the Colorado River in Utah and Colorado, and one tributary, the San Juan River in New Mexico.

The common backswimmer or water wasp makes up in fierceness for what it lacks in size. A torpedo-shaped bug just half an inch long, it swims upside down on its back, using its long back legs like oars. It is also called a water wasp because it will sometimes bite a person's bare hand or leg, mistaking it for prey. These predators sneak up on their prey—other insects and small aquatic animals—by swimming

underneath, then quickly biting. Backswimmers live in ponds and slow-flowing shallow streams throughout North America, including the Southwest.

WHERE HAVE THE RIVERS GONE? Southwest rivers and streams are endangered. Their flows shrink or disappear entirely when people take water from rivers and streams. In the Southwest, farming uses more water than any other activity, even household use. Dams also endanger Southwest rivers. Damming a river changes its flow, the water temperature, and how much silt and sand the water carries, making an entirely different habitat. In some parts of the Southwest, people are working to restore river and stream habitat by reestablishing water flows and replanting river and streamside plants.

RESTORING RIVERS. Before March 1993, the banks of the upper Gila River in southwestern New Mexico were bare and eroding. Old cottonwoods and willows had once lined the river, providing homes for animals, shading the water to keep it cool enough for fish, and preventing erosion by slowing down floodwaters. But the trees were dying out. The river was in trouble. Then, in one long day, an energetic group of kids and adults planted 300 young cottonwood and willow trees and shrubs along the riverbanks. Now one stretch of the Gila River is coming alive again.

River otter

Made in the Shade

BECAUSE TREES ARE RARE in many parts of the Southwest, they are beloved for the cool greenery and shade. Among the region's most well-loved trees are spreading cottonwoods, twisted piñon pines, and tall, straight ponderosa pines.

COTTONWOOD
PIÑON PINE
PONDEROSA PINE

Cottonwoods say "water is nearby," welcome information in this dry landscape. Tall trees with gray, furrowed bark and heart-shaped leaves that turn gold in fall, cottonwoods grow in wet soils along streams, irrigation ditches, and rivers throughout the lower elevations of the Southwest. These trees are crucial to river and streamside ecosystems. Their spreading roots hold streambank soils against erosion. Their broad branches and leafy canopies provide homes for dozens of kinds of animals, from great blue herons and eagles to orioles and web-forming caterpillars.

Southwestern peoples use cottonwood in many ways. Pueblo Indians hollow out cottonwood logs for ceremonial drums. Hopis traditionally carve kachinas—sculptures of sacred beings—from cottonwood roots. Navajos use cottonwood for prayer sticks, rug looms, and logs to build hogans—traditional eight-sided houses.

Unfortunately, as people have dried up streams and rivers throughout the Southwest, cottonwood *bosques* (say BOES-kays)—streamside woodlands—have vanished too.

Piñon pines have provided Southwesterners with their favorite firewood for centuries. In winter, Southwest towns smell of fragrant piñon smoke. Piñon pines are short, often twisted pine trees with single needles or needles in clusters of two. Of all southwestern pine trees, piñons grow in the driest environments. Because of this, piñons grow at a snail's pace. An 80- to 100-year-old piñon may be only 10 feet tall, with a trunk small enough to encircle with two hands. Piñons

COUNTING RINGS

Long-lived trees like ponderosa pines help us understand ancient climate patterns and ancient people. Each year, a tree grows a new ring of wood. Counting backwards from the year a tree died, scientists use dendrochronology—tree ring dating—to read past climate patterns. In wet years, trees grow wide rings; in dry years, the rings are narrow. Tree rings in trees cut for roof beams in cliff dwellings and other ancient buildings can be dated to tell us exactly when the buildings were built.

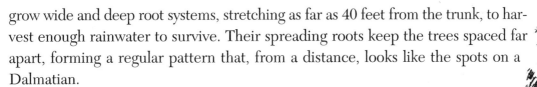

grow wide and deep root systems, stretching as far as 40 feet from the trunk, to harvest enough rainwater to survive. Their spreading roots keep the trees spaced far apart, forming a regular pattern that, from a distance, looks like the spots on a Dalmatian.

Ponderosa pines are the Southwest's tallest trees. They grow up to 120 feet tall, with trunks 3 to 4 feet across. (In wetter climates, they reach 220 feet, the height of a 20-story building!) Named for their ponderous—heavy—wood, ponderosa pines are the major lumber tree in the Southwest. Ponderosa pine wood is valued for cabinets, Southwestern-style furniture, and house trim.

YUMMY NUTS Every three to seven years, piñon pines produce a bumper crop of 2-inch-long cones holding plump, delicious seeds. Animals from tiny nut borers (insects) to big black bears—and people—harvest the nuts. Piñon nuts (sometimes called pine nuts) taste great on pizza and in brownies. If you harvest wild piñon nuts, carefully crack the brown husk to get to the edible, ivory-colored nut.

Piñon jays are blue-gray, robin-sized birds that live in flocks of up to several hundred birds. These jays fly long distances to find their main food—piñon nuts. They harvest and store tons of the piñon nuts in holes in the ground near their nesting areas. (Uneaten nuts sprout into new piñon trees.) Each jay can carry up to 20 nuts packed in its throat.

Ponderosa pine

YOU CAN DO IT!
You can identify some trees by smelling their bark. Ponderosa pine bark, for instance, smells like vanilla. Look for a tall, straight pine tree with rough, rusty orange bark. Stick your nose carefully into a crack in the bark and sniff. Does it smell like vanilla?

Cyanobacteria in desert soil

What's Underfoot?

THERE IS SO MUCH TO LOOK AT in the Southwest that you may forget to look down and see what's right under your nose.

If you get down on your knees, you may see a bumpy miniature landscape of mesas and valleys covering desert soils. This tiny topography is a cryptobiotic crust, a com-

CRYPTOBIOTIC CRUST
SLICKROCK
DESERT PAVEMENT
DESERT VARNISH

munity of creatures that glues most desert soils in place, keeping them from washing or blowing away. The tiny creatures that make up a cryptobiotic crust—some too small to be seen without a microscope—form a living web at the surface of the soil that binds the particles and helps soak up and hold precious water.

These living crusts are held together by microscopic organisms called cyanobacteria. Cyanobacteria grow inside sticky sheaths much thinner than a human hair. Their sticky casings glue together the particles of desert soil, fertilize the soil by adding nitrogen, and prevent nutrients that plants need in order to grow from washing out of the soil. Once cyanobacteria stabilize the soil, other life forms may move in, including fungal threads, green algae, and lichens and mosses.

In some parts of the Colorado Plateau in southern Utah and northern Arizona, what is underfoot is rock—bare rock. This landscape is called "slickrock," but it isn't slick

at all. Slickrock is named for the naked smoothness of the exposed rust red, orange, and ivory rock layers. These eroded sandstone layers are "fossil" sand dunes, deposited by the wind more than 200 million years ago when this part of the Southwest was a Sahara Desert–like landscape.

In windblown parts of the hottest deserts, the soil may be covered with an even surface of rounded pebbles that look as though someone laid them in a tidy pavement. Called desert pavement, this pebble surface is a result of soil movement, not people's artistry. As the soil gets wet and dries, it pushes stones up to the surface. Constant desert winds blow away the small soil particles. The heavier pebbles remain, and are rounded and polished by the winds.

The upper sides of exposed rocks in the Southwest—including pebbles in desert pavement—are often darker than the lower sides, as if the rocks are sunburned. The dark coating is actually desert varnish, a blue-black polish of clay particles and minerals. The slightly shiny layer is formed by a combination of water, wind, and microscopic creatures. Water seeps from inside the rock or trickles down cliff faces. Windblown clay particles from desert soils stick to these moist places. Microscopic fungi and bacteria living on the rock concentrate the minerals in the clay, forming the blue-black coating. Desert varnish paints dark streaks on cliffs, especially where short-lived waterfalls form after summer rains.

GONE WITH THE WIND Cryptobiotic crusts are pretty tough. But they can't stand up to trampling by lots of heavy animals, like people or cows. Cars and off-road vehicles cause serious damage too. When these living crusts break up, the soil quickly blows or washes away, leaving only the bare slickrock. Plants can't grow on bare rock, nor can animals burrow through it. You can help maintain cryptobiotic crusts by staying on established trails and roads.

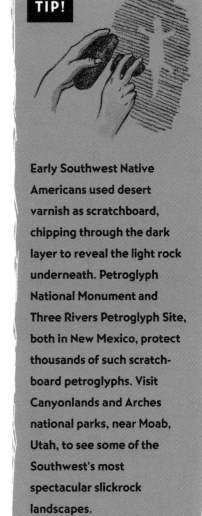

HOT TIP!

Early Southwest Native Americans used desert varnish as scratchboard, chipping through the dark layer to reveal the light rock underneath. Petroglyph National Monument and Three Rivers Petroglyph Site, both in New Mexico, protect thousands of such scratchboard petroglyphs. Visit Canyonlands and Arches national parks, near Moab, Utah, to see some of the Southwest's most spectacular slickrock landscapes.

YOU CAN DO IT! Cryptobiotic crusts seem dead much of the year, because the inhabitants are dormant—essentially in a deep sleep—when the soil is dry. But these tiny creatures come alive quickly after a rain. You can see and smell them as they return to activity. First, find an area of knobby, dry cryptobiotic soil. (Canyonlands and Arches national parks, near Moab, Utah, are good places to look.) Gently pour water on the soil to wet it. Come back in a few hours and look at your patch of soil. Does it look darker, faintly greenish? Does it smell wet and earthy?

Tricks of Hot Air

SOMETIMES, THE SOUTHWEST'S HOT, DRY AIR acts as a trickster, producing whirling columns of hot air, called dust devils, and ghostly images called mirages.

Dust devils are named for the dust that makes them visible and for their skipping, unpredictable courses. Dust devils usually whirl for only a few minutes, but they can grow as much as 100 feet tall and 20 feet across before running out of hot air. Though usually harmless, their 20- to 30-mile-per-hour winds can easily loft tumbleweeds, large lizards, trash, or even lawn chairs! Dust devils look like mini-tornadoes, but they are not. Tornadoes need moist conditions; dust devils are creatures of dry air. Nevada's Gosiute Indians believed that they were born of the windblown dust, and that whirlwinds embodied their ancestors' spirits.

DUST DEVILS MIRAGES

Dust devils or whirlwinds are creatures of the sun. When the sun shines full strength on the soil, it heats up the ground. The hot ground in turn heats a thin layer of air next to it. Eventually, a bubble of this hot air floats upward from the ground and other hot air rushes in to replace it, forming a rising stream of air called a thermal. When the thermal begins to spin, a dust devil is born.

The same layer of hot air next to the ground plays tricks on your eyes, forming mirages if it remains still. The boundary between a still layer of hot air next to the ground and the cooler air above it bends the light rays that strike it. (The boundary between air and still water does the same thing. When you dip your arm in water, it seems to "bend" just beneath the surface, even though your arm is straight.) The boundary between the two layers of air acts like a giant mirror, reflecting images.

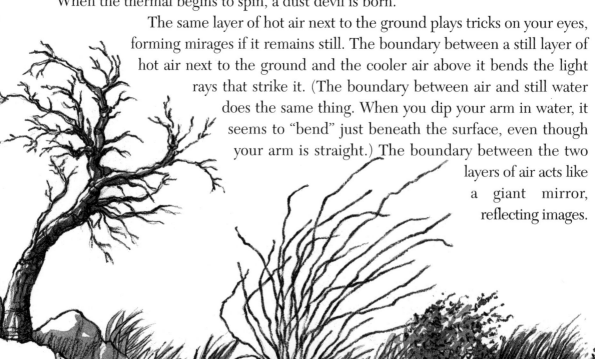

The simplest mirages occur when the "mirror" simply reflects the bright sky. These mirages paint lakes in the desert where no water occurs, or puddles on perfectly dry pavement. Such phantom lakes sometimes lured early desert travelers to thirsty deaths. Mirages also cause distant objects like mesas to look as if they float free of the surrounding landscape, separated from the land by a layer of sky. More complicated mirages copy distant landmarks upside down, so that mountains, for instance, sprout bottoms-up mirror images.

Mirages and dust devils are especially common in the deserts because they are the sunniest, driest parts of the region. During the cloudless days of spring and summer, the hot sun heats the already dry soil—perfect conditions for tricks of hot air.

GIANT WHIRLWINDS Flat basins at the Southwest's lowest elevations combine with sizzling summer temperatures to produce super dust devils. These monsters tower up to 1/2 mile high, pack winds up to 90 miles per hour, and can tear off roofs and collapse walls. On Utah's Bonneville Salt Flats, scientists tag these giants by spreading special colored dust on the ground. When a whirlwind passes, it vacuums up the surface debris, including the colored dust, "painting" its whirling form so that it is easy to track.

PHANTOM CITIES In the 1950s, residents of Yuma, in southwestern Arizona, were definitely seeing things. On hot, unusually still days, a shimmering city appeared in the desert west of Yuma. Astonished viewers could distinguish buildings with red tile roofs, a harbor with ships coming and going, and cars on the streets. They were "seeing" San Diego, California, 150 miles west on the Pacific Coast, beyond several mountain ranges. The images of San Diego were telescopic mirages. Telescopic mirages are rare because they require still air layers that cover hundreds of miles.

Dust devil

Booms and Zaps

ON A HOT, SUNNY SOUTHWEST AFTERNOON, puffy white clouds build in the blue sky like oversized cauliflower heads. Before long, the clouds have grown into towering cloud castles that block out the sun. Suddenly, a sizzling white bolt of lightning streaks earthward. Thunder rumbles. As if summoned by the sound, rain pours down, drenching everything it touches. In a few minutes, or perhaps an hour, the rain quits and the warm sun returns.

THUNDERSTORMS
LIGHTNING

The entire Southwest, from desert and canyon to mesa and mountain, shares one thing: the summer thunderstorm season, lasting from July through September. Unlike the gentle, widespread winter rains and snows, summer thunderstorms are local and intense. A storm may dump as much as 4 inches of rain in an hour in one place, while 10 miles away, the sun shines and no rain falls.

In some parts of the region, the summer rains bring as much as three-quarters of the yearly moisture. Plants come alive, growing and blooming. Because food is abundant, many Southwest animals—from tiny fairy shrimp to spadefoot toads and peccaries—bear their young during the rainy season.

Most rainy season storms are thunderstorms, with lightning and booming thunder. Lightning is a powerful electric charge that zips between cloud and ground, between cloud and cloud, or within one cloud. (Scientists have studied lightning since Benjamin Franklin flew a kite into a thunderstorm in 1752 and picked up an electric charge. But we still don't know exactly what produces the electricity that powers lightning.) Thunder is the sound made when a lightning bolt heats the air. Although an old saying holds that lightning never strikes the same place twice, multiple lightning flashes often travel precisely the same path through

DANGER!
On August 12, 1992, a professor at New Mexico Tech in Socorro was struck and killed by lightning while he was dashing across an open area on the college campus during a thunderstorm. Many more people die each year after being struck by lightning than are killed by bites of rattlesnakes or other venomous animals. To avoid being zapped, stay away from open areas, antennae, electrical appliances, and tall trees during thunderstorms. Lightning often strikes the tallest object around. If you are standing nearby, the bolt can hit you too. Take shelter inside a building, under a cliff overhang, or in a car.

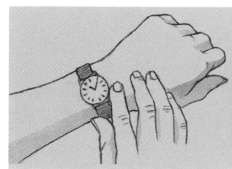

YOU CAN DO IT!
To measure how far away from you a lightning strike is, use a watch to count how many seconds pass from when you see the lightning until you hear the thunder. Divide the number of seconds by five. The result is the number of miles away from the lightning hit. (The sound of thunder travels at the speed of sound, two-tenths of a mile per second.)

the air, striking the same spot many times. The repeating flashes speed so quickly that they look like one flash.

Cimarron, in the Sangre de Cristo Mountains of northern New Mexico, is the lightning and thunderstorm capital of the United States, averaging more than 110 days with thunderstorms each year. Located where the heights of the Rocky Mountains rise from the flat expanse of the Great Plains, Cimarron has plenty of the warm, moist, unstable air that spawns thunderstorms.

CELEBRATING THE RAIN Many Southwest peoples perform ceremonies to ask the rainclouds to bring their life-giving waters, or simply to celebrate the rainy season's arrival. In late June, traditional Hispanic communities bless the fields on San Juan's Day. Around the same time, the Sonoran Desert–dwelling O'odham of southern Arizona and northern Sonora, Mexico, harvest saguaro and organ pipe cactus fruit and call up the rains. Pueblo and Hopi villages hold rain dances throughout the summer. Ancient people called up the rains, too. Petroglyphs showing a bird flying upward to pierce a raincloud with its beak are believed to be prayers for rain.

SUDDEN WATERS Never hike, bike, or drive in arroyos (dry stream channels) during a thunderstorm. Flash floods, which bring torrents of rushing water, and soil, rocks, and other debris, can suddenly sweep down arroyos during or after heavy rains. Flash floods can tear down whole trees, sweep away cars or even houses, and certainly drown people. (More people die in flash floods each year in the Southwest than are killed by venomous animals.) In fact, stay out of arroyo channels if you see thunderclouds in the sky, even if it isn't raining where you are.

Endangered Species

An endangered species is a plant or animal that biologists fear is about to become extinct. Endangered species—and threatened species (plants and animals that may become endangered)—are protected by law.

Why preserve endangered or threatened species? Each plant and animal is important. From tiny, single-celled algae to quarter-ton grizzly bears, each creature plays a crucial role in keeping its ecosystem stable and healthy.

Ecosystems are like huge webs made up of interconnections of many animals and plants and their landscapes. When all of the strands of the web are intact and strong, the web works well. When one strand is broken, the web is weakened. And when many strands are broken, the web begins to disintegrate.

In the Southwest, for example, the disappearance of the willow flycatcher points out that its home in the forests along rivers and streams is disappearing also. This, in turn, tells us that many Southwest rivers and streams are in trouble. The webs of life that make up earth's ecosystems are our home, too, providing us with food, shelter, clean air, and water—as well as beauty. If earth's ecosystems disintegrate, where will we go?

There are other reasons to preserve endangered species. For instance, one-fourth of the world's medicines, from aspirin to brand-new cancer-fighting drugs, were originally discovered in wild plants and animals. Who knows what future medicines we might lose as we lose species? Another reason to preserve endangered species is simply because they exist. When these unique creatures and plants are gone, there will be nothing like them on earth again. Sometimes we don't understand how important a species is until it is gone.

Everyone can make a difference. Find out about the endangered or threatened species in your area and what is being done to protect them. Write letters, become involved with cleanup or replanting efforts. Show that you care about the world you live in!

HOW DOES IT HAPPEN? Plants and animals may become endangered or threatened when their habitat is so changed that they can no longer survive. Or they may become endangered because people kill them. And some plants and animals become endangered because their habitat is naturally limited. Often, species become endangered for more than one of these reasons.

The Colorado squawfish became endangered when dams changed stretches of the Colorado River from swift-flowing water to still reservoirs. The temperature of the water, and the amount of oxygen and sediment in it, also changed. The habitat of the

river was so altered that the Colorado squawfish now only survive in a few short stretches of the river.

Mexican gray wolves once roamed the mountains, plains, and mesas of the Southwest, hunting elk, moose, and bison in packs. By the 1930s, they had disappeared from the wild—trapped, shot, or poisoned by people. Today, just over 50 Mexican gray wolves survive in captivity, and biologists are trying to build up their populations so that wolves can live in wild areas of the Southwest again.

And Knowlton's cactus, a 1-inch, many-stemmed cactus, grows only on one mesa in northwestern New Mexico. This tiny species is rare because its habitat is limited. Collectors so prized this rare plant that by 1979 there were few plants left. Fortunately the cactus is now protected, and botanists are working to replant Knowlton's cactus.

Mexican gray wolf

The Wild Inside

Whether you need someplace to go on a rainy day in the Southwest or want a closer look at the natural and cultural history of the region, check out these extra-special places for kids of all ages.

- In southwestern Colorado, don't miss the **Anasazi Heritage Center** east of Dolores. It includes a full-scale replica of an archaeological trench, interactive computer programs, and drawers of "touch me" artifacts. Free. Phone: (303) 882-4811.

- Walk through a life-size, six-room replica of an Anasazi (ancient ones) house at **Anasazi Indian Village State Park** near Boulder in southern Utah. Walk a trail through the excavated village. Fee. Phone: (801) 335-7308.

- The **Arizona–Sonora Desert Museum**, west of Tucson, Arizona, ranks as the best nature museum in the Southwest. Includes habitat exhibits with prairie dog burrows into which kids can look, underwater windows to view frolicking otters, and a walk-in hummingbird aviary. Fee. Phone: (520) 883-2702.

- At **Crow Canyon Archaeological Center**, just north of Cortez, Colorado, you can participate in a working archaeological dig. Fee. Prior reservations required. Phone: (303) 565-8975 or (800) 422-8975.

- The **Indian Pueblo Cultural Center** in Albuquerque, New Mexico, gives a fascinating view of Pueblo Indian life. Includes a children's area, restaurant featuring traditional Pueblo foods, and weekend dances and crafts demonstrations. Fee. Phone: (505) 843-7270 or 800-766-4405.

- The **Las Cruces Museum of Natural History** in southern New Mexico is small, but exceptionally kid-oriented. Many innovative hands-on exhibits; some live animals. Donation. Phone: (505) 522-3120.

- The **Museum of Northern Arizona** is the place to learn about the people and natural environments of the Colorado Plateau. Great hands-on exhibits. Visit the gift shop for kid-friendly prices on authentic Native American art. Fee. Phone: (520) 774-5211.

- Dinosaur fanatics will love the **New Mexico Museum of Natural History** in Albuquerque, New Mexico. Includes life-size dinosaur models, a walk-through volcano, an ice-age cave replica, and a "time machine." Fee. Phone: (505) 841-8837.

Wild Books

Do you want to know more about the Southwest? These are some of my favorite books on the region.

■ *And It Is Still That Way*, Bird Baylor (Trails West Publishing, 1976). A wonderful collection of legends told by Arizona Native American children.

■ *The Boy Who Made Dragonfly*, Tony Hillerman (University of New Mexico Press, 1972). A beautiful Zuni myth retold by the dean of Southwest mystery writers. Includes thoughtful interpretive notes on Zuni culture.

■ *The Great Southwest Nature Factbook*, Susan J. Tweit (Alaska Northwest Books, 1992). A browser's guide to animals, plants, and natural features in the Southwest.

■ *Hiking the Southwest's Canyon Country*, Sandra Hinchman (The Mountaineers, 1990). Just covers the Colorado Plateau, but an excellent guide with emphasis on taking children along.

■ *Insects of the Southwest*, Floyd Werner and Carol Olson (Fisher Books, 1994). Also not written specifically for kids, but quite charming and full of fascinating information.

■ *Mushrooms and Truffles of the Southwest*, Jack S. States (University of Arizona Press, 1990). Not written specifically for kids, but has nice color photographs. Also includes information on lichens.

■ *The Sierra Club Guides to the National Parks: Desert Southwest*, Irene Pavitt, project editor (Stewart, Tabori & Chang, 1984). Also for adults, but a good resource for natural history and geology information.

■ *Skywatch: A Western Weather Guide*, Richard A. Keen (Fulcrum, 1987). All the weather information you could want. A little advanced for younger kids, but includes fascinating lists of facts.

■ *Smithsonian Guide to Historic America: The Desert States*, Michael S. Durham (Stewart, Tabori & Chang, 1990). For adults, but full of fun historical stories that kids will appreciate.

■ *Taking the Kids: To the Great American Southwest*, Eileen Ogintz (HarperCollins West, 1994). A kids-eye view of travel in the United States Southwest. A note of caution: use common sense with suggested kid's activities; some could be dangerous.

Wild Checklist

As you travel throughout the Southwest, it's fun to keep track of the plants, animals, natural features and phenomena, and the important places that you see and experience. You'll be amazed at how much you will see of the wild Southwest around you!

PLANTS

___Agave
___Aspen
___Buffalo gourd
___Cholla cactus
___Cottonwood
___Creosote
___Devil's claw
___Fly agaric **POISONOUS**
___Gambel oak
___Goatsbeard
___Monkeyflower
___Paintbrush
___Piñon pine
___Ponderosa pine
___Prickly pear
___Sacred datura **POISONOUS**
___Sagebrush
___Saguaro cactus
___Saltcedar
___Tumbleweed
___Water hemlock **POISONOUS**
___Wildflowers
___Wild raspberry
___Yucca

ANIMALS
Birds

___Buteo
___Cactus wren
___Canyon wren
___Dove

___Falcon
___Golden eagle
___Harris's hawk
___Hummingbird
___Magpie
___Northern mockingbird
___Owl
___Piñon jay
___Quail
___Raven
___Roadrunner
___Vulture
___White-throated swift

Bugs

___Ant
___Black widow spider
___Centipede
___Digger bee
___Dragonfly
___Fire ant
___Grasshopper
___Millipede
___Scorpion
___Sphinx moth
___Tarantula spider
___Termite
___Velvet ant

Lizards, Snakes, Frogs, Fish

___Collared lizards
___Colorado squawfish **ENDANGERED**
___Common backswimmer

___Fairy shrimp

___Gila monster

___Horned lizard

___Leopard frog

___Rattlesnake

___Spadefoot toad

___Tiger salamander

___Whiptail lizard

Mammals and Other Animals

___Bat

___Bighorn sheep

___Black bear

___Burro

___Coyote

___Desert cottontail

___Desert tortoise

___Jackrabbit

___Kangaroo rat

___Mountain lion

___Mule deer

___Packrat

___Peccary

___Pika

___Porcupine

___Prairie dog

___Pronghorn

___River otter

___Snowshoe hare

___White-tailed deer

NATURAL FEATURES AND PHENOMENA

___Arch

___Arroyo

___Balanced rock

___Cliff dwelling

___Cryptobiotic crust

___Desert pavement

___Desert varnish

___Dinosaur tracks

___Dust devil

___Fin

___Flash flood

___Hoodoo

___Lightning

___Mirage

___Natural bridge

___Petroglyphs

___Pictographs

___Slickrock

___Thunderstorm

IMPORTANT PLACES

___Ácoma Pueblo, New Mexico

___Alkimel O'odham Reservation, Arizona

___Canyon de Chelly, Arizona

___Casas Grandes, Mexico

___Chaco Canyon, New Mexico

___Chihuahuan Desert

___Cliff Palace at Mesa Verde National Park, Colorado

___Desert Botanical Garden, Phoenix, Arizona

___Four Corners

___Goosenecks of the San Juan, Utah

___Gila River

___Great Basin Desert

___Mojave Desert

___Narrows of the Virgin River in Zion National Park, Utah

___Newspaper Rock, Utah

___North Rim of the Grand Canyon, Arizona

___Old Oraibi, Arizona

___Rainbow Bridge, Utah-Arizona border
___Rio Grande River
___Robbers Roost in Canyonlands National Park, Utah
___Shiprock, New Mexico
___Sonoran Desert
___Zuni Pueblo

NATIONAL PARKS, MONUMENTS, AND WILDLIFE REFUGES

___Arches National Park, Utah
___Big Bend National Park, Texas
___Bryce Canyon National Park, Utah
___Cabeza Prieta National Wildlife Refuge, Arizona
___Canyonlands National Park, Utah
___Carlsbad Caverns National Park, New Mexico
___Casa Grande Ruins National Monument, Arizona
___Chaco Culture National Historical Park, New Mexico
___Chiricahua National Monument, Arizona
___El Malpaís National Monument, New Mexico
___Grand Canyon National Park, Arizona
___Hovenweep National Monument, Colorado
___Mesa Verde National Park, Colorado
___Natural Bridges National Monument, Utah
___Organ Pipe Cactus National Monument, Arizona
___Petrified Forest National Park, Arizona
___Petroglyph National Monument, New Mexico
___Saguaro National Park, Arizona
___Three Rivers Petroglyph Site, New Mexico
___White Sands National Monument, New Mexico
___Zion National Park, Utah

State Parks

___Anasazi Indian Village State Park, Utah
___City of Rocks State Park, New Mexico
___Goblin Valley State Reserve, Utah
___Rockhound State Park, New Mexico

Tribal Parks

___Monument Valley Tribal Park, Arizona

The Southwest is home to over three dozen Native American groups. The many reservations range from the Navajo Reservation in northern Arizona, northeastern New Mexico, and southeastern Utah—stretching over an area larger than the state of Massachusetts—to the tiny community of Ysleta Pueblo outside El Paso, Texas.

Wild Words

ADAPT—to be able to adjust to changing conditions and to function. Coyotes have adapted to changing conditions by learning to find new kinds of food in towns and cities.

AMPHIBIAN—an animal that is able to live both on land and in water. Frogs, toads, and salamanders are all amphibians.

AQUATIC—a plant or animal that grows or lives in water. Tadpoles are the aquatic young of frogs.

BACTERIA—a kind of microscopic creature. Bacteria are found everywhere in the world, including the stomachs of cows and between grains of soil.

CACTI—plural of cactus. Cacti are fleshy plants with spines instead of leaves.

CAMOUFLAGE—to hide. Horned lizards camouflage themselves by looking like small rocks.

CLONE—something that is an exact copy. Aspen trees in a grove look alike because each is a clone—an exact copy of the parent.

DEHYDRATE—to lose water or take water from. If you don't drink enough water, your body will become dehydrated.

ECOSYSTEM—A group of living and nonliving things and their environment.

Each part of an ecosystem, whether an animal, plant, rock, or the weather, is important because it interacts with the other parts.

ENVIRONMENT—the larger world in which a creature lives. The earth is the only environment in our solar system that supports human life.

EVAPORATE—when a liquid changes to vapor. A puddle of water evaporates in the heat of the sun.

EVOLVE—the process when a living being changes permanently in response to changes in its environment. Over thousands of years as the deserts dried out and became warmer, cacti evolved spines instead of leaves.

EXCRETE—to give off. Poisonous snakes excrete venom.

FERAL—A domestic animal living in the wild. Feral horses can survive in the desert only where there are water holes.

FUNGUS—a kind of plant that doesn't make its own food from sunlight; instead it feeds on other plants or decaying material. Mushrooms and molds are both fungi (plural of fungus).

GERMINATE— to sprout. Desert wildflower seeds germinate after spring rains.

HABITAT—the specific place where a

plant or animal lives in nature. Streams and ponds are beaver habitats.

LARVA—The young stage or stages of an animal that goes through metamorphosis. The larval stage of some winged insects often don't have wings.

MAMMAL—an animal that has a backbone, nurses its young (feeds its young milk), and has body hair. Humans are mammals, and so are peccaries.

METABOLISM—the processes by which a living creature burns food for energy and gets rid of inedible waste. A hummingbird's metabolism is very high; it must eat frequently.

METAMORPHOSIS—a dramatic change in structure or appearance, such as the metamorphosis of a tadpole into a frog.

MICROSCOPIC—very tiny; something so small that it can only be seen through a microscope. Cyanobacterial threads are microscopic.

NOCTURNAL—active at night. Bats are nocturnal animals; they hunt at night.

ORGANISM—a living being. An organism can be as small as a single cell or as big as a ponderosa pine tree.

PESTICIDES—chemicals that kill creatures considered to be pests. Farmers often use pesticides to kill insects that eat their crops, but other animals may be killed by eating the insects sprayed with pesticides.

PETRIFIED—plant or animal matter that has turned into stone. Whole trees buried in mudflows are slowly petrified when minerals replace their tissue.

PREDATOR—an animal that hunts and eats other animals. Owls are predators of small rodents, such as mice.

PREY—an animal that is eaten by a predator. Mice are an owl's prey.

SOLSTICE—the time of year when the sun is the farthest north or the farthest south of the equator. In the northern hemisphere, the shortest day of the year occurs when the sun is the farthest south of the equator around December 22 (winter solstice); the longest day of the year is when the sun is farthest north, around June 22 (summer solstice).

SPECIES—the basic unit in biological classification, in which all the organisms are closely related. Mountain lions and cougars are actually the same species.

SUCCULENT—Fleshy and full of water. Cactus stems are succulent.

THERMAL—relating to or caused by heat. In the desert, a thermal is a rising stream of hot air, which, if conditions are right, can turn into a dust devil.

TOXIC—poisonous. Harvester ant stings hurt because the ant's stinger contains a toxic substance.

VENOM—poison. Snakes that excrete poison are called venomous snakes.

Index

Numbers that appear in **boldface** indicate pages with illustrations.

ABOUT THE AUTHOR

Susan J. Tweit lives in the Chihuahuan Desert of southern New Mexico with her husband, Richard Cabe, her stepdaughter, Molly Cabe, and one cat, Hypoteneuse. She is a naturalist, radio commentator, and the author of four books, including *The Great Southwest Nature Factbook* (Alaska Northwest Books, 1992) and *Barren, Wild, and Worthless: Living in the Chihuahuan Desert* (University of New Mexico Press, 1995). Her essays and stories have appeared in *Harrowsmith Country Life, New Mexico, Sierra, Cricket, Bloomsbury Review*, and other magazines. In her spare time, she takes long walks along the irrigation canal near her home, reads mysteries, works in her garden, and co-directs the Border Book Festival. She loves to tell stories about the desert.

ABOUT THE ILLUSTRATOR

Joyce Bergen shares her Seattle home with her husband, Larry Lund, and two cats, Phoebe and Baby Ruth. She regularly illustrates plants and animals for exhibits and publications. Her work appears in The Nature Conservancy's *Preserving Washington Wildlands* (1993), and at the Woodland Park Zoo of Seattle, Oregon Coast Aquarium, New Orleans Aquarium of the Americas, and Riverbanks Zoo of South Carolina. Joyce is happiest when she's out hiking, cross-country skiing, or just wandering around hoping to see an animal. Her positively best vacations were all spent roaming the deserts of the Southwest.

WILD NOTES

WILD NOTES

WILD NOTES

WILD NOTES

WILD NOTES

WILD NOTES

WILD NOTES

WILD NOTES

WILD NOTES

WILD NOTES

WILD NOTES

WILD NOTES